the Wager
Donna Jo Napoli

HENRY HOLT AND COMPANY
NEW YORK

Henry Holt and Company, LLC
Publishers since 1866
175 Fifth Avenue
New York, New York 10010
www.HenryHoltKids.com

Distributed in Canada by H. B. Fenn and Company Ltd.

Library of Congress Cataloging-in-Publication Data
Napoli, Donna Jo.
The wager / Donna Jo Napoli.—1st ed.
p. cm.
Summary: Having lost everything in a tidal wave in 1169 Sicily, nineteen-year-old Don Giovanni makes a simple-sounding wager with a stranger he recognizes as the devil but, while desperate enough to surrender his pride and good looks for three years, he is not willing to give up his soul.
ISBN 978-0-8050-8781-9
[1. Conduct of life—Fiction. 2. Wagers—Fiction. 3. Aristocracy (Social class)—Fiction. 4. Pride and vanity—Fiction. 5. Devil—Fiction. 6. Don Juan (Legendary character)—Fiction. 7. Sicily (Italy)—History—1016–1194—Fiction. 8. Italy—History—12th century—Fiction.] I. Title.
PZ7.N15Wag 2010 [Fic]—dc22 2009023436

First Edition—2010
Printed in March 2010 in the United States of America by
R.R. Donnelley & Sons Company, Harrisonburg, Virginia

1 3 5 7 9 10 8 6 4 2

For

JACK ZIPES,

with gratitude for his wonderful books
and generous friendship

the Wager

Messina, 1169

DON GIOVANNI LOOKED OUT THE CASTLE WINDOW OVER THE strait that separated the island of Sicily from the mainland. He fingered the fine silk of his shirtsleeves and smiled. "The sea is bluer because it's mine."

"Don't be absurd."

He turned. A maidservant carried a tray into the room. The scent of honey and sheep's milk ricotta promised such sweet satisfaction that his smile lingered, despite her words. He tilted his head. "What did you say?"

"You heard me." Her attention was on the heavy tray.

Reckless woman. Girl, actually, judging by the skin on the back of her olive hands. Her arms were long under those thin brown sleeves. Shapely, in fact. A fine girl. He spoke coolly: "I'm giving you a chance to retract."

She set the tray on the table. "No one owns the sea."

Heat rose up Don Giovanni's neck. He looked out the window again. If he stood just so, with his body slightly turned, the window well was thick enough that it blocked his view of the city of Messina; all he saw was his own property. "I own everything in sight. The sea is mine."

"You really are ridiculous."

He walked over with large steps and snapped his fingers in her face. "How dare you speak to me like that!"

"If you talk like a fool, you deserve it." She arranged bowls on the table, never raising her eyes.

Don Giovanni blinked in disbelief. He wished the maid would lift her face so he could get a better view. She was familiar in a vague sort of way. Angela or Angiola or Annetta or Andriana or something like that. Some openmouthed name that resounded in the head. Bah, there were too many servants to keep track. He put his hand out to stay hers. "You're finished," he said. "Leave."

"Are you firing me?"

"If you talk like a fool, you deserve it," he said.

"A *gran signore*—a big don—more like a big clown." The maid wiped her hands brusquely on her apron and left.

It was astonishing enough that she'd spoken so rudely, but for her simply to leave after being fired was beyond understanding. She should have fallen to her knees, professed regret, cried on his shoes. Even kissed them.

He would have forgiven her magnanimously. Despite her sarcasm, he was, indeed, a *gran signore*. Don Giovanni's parents had died when he was thirteen. All their earthly possessions had gone to him, as their only heir. Don Alfinu, a neighbor and family friend, guided and counseled Giovanni. He made sure the boy continued his studies of Greek and Arabic, and he added French. Greek, because it gave access to cultured literature and, to be practical, because so many in northeastern Sicily spoke it. Arabic, because it gave access to scientific literature and, of course, because merchants spoke it. And French, because it was essential for a role in public life. Don Alfinu was grooming Giovanni to be the most important political figure of Messina. And since Messina was the second-largest city in Sicily, the king, in Palermo, would naturally consult Don Giovanni on matters affecting the whole island.

But Don Alfinu was mean-spirited; his actions were measured, nothing like the exuberant exaggerations of Giovanni's parents. Why, the boy's father used to burst into song at the sight of a split ripe watermelon. His mother pinned yellow orchids in her hair and danced in the courtyard bare-breasted in summer rain.

The orphaned boy nearly lost his mind listening to Don Alfinu drone on about loyalty to the pope and proper sexual behavior. All so restrictive and boring. So on his eighteenth birthday he'd taken control of his own property, his own destiny. He'd assumed the title of don and become a baron overnight. He gave lavish parties that everyone wanted to be invited to—and everyone was. He lent money freely. Don Alfinu ranted, calling him a wastrel, so Don Giovanni stopped visiting the old nag.

Everyone had heard of Don Giovanni's generosity of spirit and purse. They admired him.

Or should. That maidservant was intolerable.

Now the mistress of the servants came in. He knew her name at least: Betta. She held her head high, and the ropes of her neck stood out. She was trailed by more maidservants carrying trays. She lit the many candles.

Don Giovanni backed to the wall and watched the table fill with dried white figs from the Lipari Islands—the very best kind—and cheeses, toasted pine nuts, bowls of coconut shreds. The profusion of colors and scents made the air above the table shimmer in the candle glow. His eyes glazed over. He felt tipsy. Maybe he was ill?

He rubbed his cheeks. Had anyone heard the girl abuse him? If so, he'd demand a public apology. Don Giovanni had to protect an impeccable reputation. He had plans. Don Alfinu's complaints about his spending had gotten so strident lately, they worried him. So he'd invited everyone tonight for an extravagant gala to squelch any nascent rumor that his wealth might be dwindling. That way, when he went to borrow money to buy the land he wanted along the north coast, everyone would open their coffers without hesitation. Don Giovanni would increase his holdings and become the undisputed master of northeastern Sicily. He'd surpass Don Alfinu's expectations, but—more important—he'd do it his own way, by being the richest, not the strictest.

This mistress was the most likely one to have overheard that distasteful exchange with the maidservant.

"Where are the Arab dishes?" he asked her abruptly.

"Eggplants preserved under vinegar with capers, excellent sire." Betta opened her heavily lined palm toward a silver platter. "A superb Arab dish. And over here . . ." She opened the other palm. ". . . fried mullets with onions in cane sugar. A North African dish of Saracen origin."

The words were delivered cleanly. Nothing mocked.

She walked to the end of the table, her long skirts swaying with the extreme motion of her hips. An unexpected seduction? "Roasted rabbit with raisins and almonds, a dish those Viking-hearted Normans took credit for." Betta gave him a closed-lip smile, discreet. "But we know our people have made that since the start of time. As common as fried squid." Her hand swept the area. "Over here, tiny lamb meatballs. A recipe from Palermo Jews." With a sigh, she locked her hands, the fingers of one slipping under the fingers of the other, in front of her chest. Elbows pointed down, like broken wings. She was a waiting bird. "A proper table for our grand Sicilian don."

Don Giovanni flinched at her last words. He narrowed his eyes. But Betta fussed with the decorative pine needles and holly boughs full of dried red berries. She stepped back for an admiring assessment, then hurried off.

There was nothing suspect in what she'd said. It was truth: Don Giovanni was a man of great spirit, who welcomed people of every faith into his home. In Sicily's past, nasty things had happened: Muslim shops were pillaged, Jews driven from their homes. But nothing like that would happen these days, not anywhere near Don Giovanni's castle.

So Betta's words were sincere—and no one had witnessed the earlier maidservant's insolence.

He glanced out the window over the strait. The sea lay flat. Dead. Well, what a strange way to think of it. It was calm, peaceful. A good sea. His sea, by God.

He blinked. A lone figure walked the beach. A woman. She looked back, upward toward Don Giovanni's castle.

A woman alone in the evening? Maybe he knew her. Don Giovanni had already enjoyed the company of many women, the kind who might walk alone at night, but not for long. They flocked to him because he was the most handsome youth of Messina, everyone agreed. Don Giovanni's prowess as a lover was growing legendary. He might even adopt Muslim ways and take a harem, like in the royal palace in Palermo.

Hmmm. Forget that beach walker. She could be a mirage, after all. The Strait of Messina was famous for the Fata Morgana, a mirage of men, horses, ships, all kinds of things. This could easily be a new trick of the waters.

Don Giovanni reached out to close the shutters.

But, wait, what was the woman doing now? Shedding an outer garment. Now her dress. Her undershift. The woman stood naked in this February chill. Exposed and vulnerable, like an opened oyster. Don Giovanni swallowed the saliva that gathered under his tongue. Her abundance impressed him. She waded into the water.

His heart went quiet. His arms fell to his sides. His breath came sour. Night swimming was dangerous, especially in the cold. He should stop her.

But the sea was calm. And he was host; already the clomp of hooves came, the clack of wooden wheels on stone.

How strangely this evening was beginning: three women, each capturing his attentions in her own way, each unreachable in her own way. Like a curse.

Nonsense. He was irresistible to women.

With the tip of a knife he popped a slice of orange into his mouth—refreshingly sour winter fruit—and went to the entrance hall to greet his guests.

His parties were known for elaborate banquets and dramatic spectacles. They rivaled the king's in Palermo. Don Giovanni knew this, for he had been a guest at the palace twice in the past year. King William II was himself just a boy, two and a half years younger than Don Giovanni. But the king gave sumptuous parties. Yet still Don Giovanni outdid him.

Tonight would be magnificent. Festivities until dawn.

Don Giovanni heard his heels click on the stone floors. Clomp and clack outside; click inside. All was fine.

But a gray form seemed to accompany him, at the very periphery of his vision. When he turned quickly to catch a full view, it disappeared. Nevertheless, he knew: it was the outline of the woman entering the water. A suicide?

But surely she wasn't dead yet. He could run down to the beach and call out. He could send a servant in a boat. Or do it himself. A Catholic soul that died by her own hand would be condemned forever. He owed it to her.

These things clattered through his head, like birds caught in a closed room, all the while his guests arriving. Their cheeks brushed both of his as they kissed the air beside him. Ladies in brightly colored satins, damasks, brocades, silks, all with many buttons; gentlemen in breeches and tight linen hose, with jewels embellishing their shirts—they filed in noisily. Gaily colored birds.

The mistress of the servants was a bird. Don Giovanni's thoughts were birds. The nobles of Messina were birds. What was happening that he kept seeing the same images? Common people said birds in a house were bad luck—and though Don Giovanni was far from common, the images still annoyed him. And three again.

Woozy once more, he leaned against the wall.

Throughout the evening Don Giovanni raised his hands to clap when others did. During the comedians' acts he laughed when others did. But he didn't hear a single thing. The clomps, clacks, clicks of earlier were gone. It was as though his ears had filled with oil, as though the oil overflowed down chest and back, as though he swam in oil.

Was the naked woman swimming?

Several times he passed the open window. The wooly bodies of sheep formed slate-gray ground clouds on the hillside. Beyond them the woman's clothes remained in a charcoal-gray heap on the beach. And there were so many stars. Billions of stars. Over a dead sea.

Until one time, close to morning, the sea wasn't dead. It trembled. Rain fell in sudden, heavy slaps. Lightning cut the clouds. Thunder drummed, waking Don Giovanni's sense of hearing. And then the earth itself trembled. Faintly, but he felt it for sure. He cried out.

Gentlemen and ladies rushed to the seaside windows and threw open the shutters, jabbering. Roofs shook, walls fell, stones on the pathways bounced. The sea pulled away from the shore, as though sucked into a monstrous mouth.

In an instant the sea bottom lay exposed as far as Don Giovanni could see. The rain ceased; the new sun's fingers grasped at the world. Marine creatures glistened in the slime that moved with their struggles. Fish flopped in the open air. Skeletons of wrecked boats stuck up obscenely.

Cries of pain, wails of grief threaded the air. City people picked their way through rubble, calling out to loved ones.

Don Giovanni's guests rushed to their homes. He watched the shore from his window as people pointed to the fish gasping. Groups hurried to gather them, reap the easy harvest. Children and fishermen and old people and women in rags. They cluttered the seabed.

He strained to see through the early light. He looked for a woman's body.

His sea was gone. He felt bereft.

What a stupid thought. It would return. And in a flash he understood. Oh, God in Heaven. He shouted warning. Already he saw the colossal wave coming. Taller than any Don Giovanni had ever seen, taller than any anyone had ever seen. And coming faster, too.

Disaster

EARTHQUAKES WERE ENDEMIC TO SICILIAN HISTORY. PHOENI-cians, Greeks, Romans, Barbarians, Byzantines, Saracens, Vikings—all came and went, but earthquakes were constant. Everyone had lived through recent small ones and everyone had heard tales about past big ones.

This one was different, though. It had to be. Past earth-quakes couldn't have brought waves like that, or the people of Messina would have known better. Some ancient knowledge lodged in their brains would have sent them scrambling up the mounts instead of rushing to the seabed.

Don Giovanni couldn't be sure how many were swept away over the city walls. Hundreds, maybe. And from the look of those crumpled homes, hundreds more died inside.

He stood stunned, rays of sunlight pinning him in place.

The enormity of the disaster came at him in rational, ordered thoughts. No confusion or fear or grief. The raw comprehension left him nearly numb, in fact.

He'd felt like this before, when he was a boy, when he heard the news of his parents' death. The three of them—father, mother, son—had visited the Mountain, the huge volcano Etna, after an eruption. Rich families flocked there to see the path of destruction left by the lava flow. It was safe by then—the volcano was settling back to sleep. They had arrived close to nightfall and stayed in the home of friends.

The three of them had stood at a window, like Don Giovanni was doing now, and watched sparkles of red slice through the dark from the southernmost crater. Spectacular, and even more so because only a week before the eruption a blizzard had coated the Mountain—a blizzard in July. The most distant craters still glistened white all the way down the slopes, in a drama of contrasts. Don Giovanni put one arm around his mother's waist, the other around his father's, and nestled there in the glory of nature's bestiality. He recognized it. He was on the cusp of adolescence—of his own bestiality. The metaphor of the moment hadn't escaped this well-educated boy. The pungent smell, like rotten eggs; the powdery feel of the ash-laden air; the sting to eyes and nose. Excruciatingly enticing.

He woke in the morning to a hand shaking his shoulder. He opened his eyes and the first sight he saw through the open window were two yellow butterflies. His mother had told him Etna was a butterfly wonderland. He rolled onto his back and faced the frightened old woman, who helped him dress. A priest came in, flanked by the owners of that home. The mistress cried. The priest's face was stricken. He talked with sympathy; his voice rocked. It came through to the boy as intoning, like in the Holy Mass. His parents had gone out to view the sparks again before dawn washed away the extremes of color. A huge flaming ball of magma shot through the sky and struck them dead, though they were hundreds of meters from the crater. Such things happened. It was the will of God. There was nothing to be done.

Nothing to be done. He hated those words. He hated that thought. Not then, but later—in retrospect.

No, Don Giovanni hadn't reacted then, and he didn't react now. It was as though time had stopped. The air of his castle pressed hard and hard and harder; his breathing went shallow; he wondered, without any trace of panic, if the pressure would grow so great he'd explode; blood would erupt from the top of his head.

Rain came. Not a storm, like before, just sweet rain.

Don Giovanni leaned from the window to let the water kiss his cheeks. But this water didn't kiss; it jabbed.

He jumped back and shook his head. His castle had been spared. He rushed to the windows that looked north. Then west, then south. He ran from window to window, searching for the homes of his guests the evening before, perched on high points, like his own. He could see several—he could reassure himself of their safety.

But the city below was ravaged. And all but the highest farmlands were ruined. Doors, roofs, furniture, boats, livestock, and bodies dangled from treetops, where the raging water had deposited them as it retreated.

How long had he been doing nothing? Long enough to be sure that the sea wouldn't come back—like some hellish ball of flames. It was already nothing more than a sloshing tide, trickling away. The surface of the water in the harbor bounced gently. No boats in sight. The entire fishing fleet had disappeared. Gone with the sea.

He raced outside and down the footpath to the nearest gate of the city. He stopped at the first wrecked house and helped the family lug stones and wood. They worked at a furious pace; fingers and knuckles bled as they dug into the ragged rubble. Eyes and ears strained for signs of life. They cradled the dying. They wept over the dead.

The rain stopped and the sun came out like a mis-timed blessing. Light reflected off puddles, intensifying the ironic sense of glory.

Don Giovanni lined up bodies for burial. He wasn't sure he knew any of the dead, stuck there in the hardening mud. Was this the man who brought firewood last week? Perhaps if the fellow hadn't been so crushed, Don Giovanni might have had a better chance at recognizing him.

When all were accounted for, he went on to the next home, and the home after that.

All the while church bells rang. Priests led processions in and out of the streets, holding sacred saints' relics and praying for the living and the dead.

It was late afternoon, and Don Giovanni was staring in dismay at the shattered leg of the man he had just rescued, when a young woman passed. She moved so quickly, all he saw was a high cheekbone, but ah, what a cheekbone. Her apron strings flew behind. Her winter shawl wrapped around her at least twice, but, still, he felt sure her body was lithe. And he caught a momentary glimpse of the back of an ankle—a slim, furtive animal his hands itched to hold.

Blood caked on Don Giovanni's clothes. A sleeve was ripped. Sweat stuck the silk of his shirt to his chest and back. His hands were raw from lifting rock. He reeked of blood, sweat, vomit. But he was still the handsomest youth of Messina. He dared anyone to challenge that. One look at his face was enough for any woman. And, despite all that had happened, his temples throbbed with desire.

So he followed her.

She raced along the footpath into the heart of town, skirting around rubble. Her hair hung loose, black, and wavy, and thick with clumps of something. Seaweed?

Don Giovanni ran now.

But each time the girl turned a corner, by the time he got there she was already turning another. No matter how much he sped up, she stayed the same distance ahead. Maddening. He was exhausted as it was—no sleep all night and then all that work, all the suffering he'd witnessed. Plus he'd missed his midday meal—and that was the most hearty meal of the day. He was in no mood for her shenanigans. He shouted to her to wait.

"Don't shout, you ass."

Don Giovanni stopped. An old crone stood in the doorway arch to a home that had crumbled behind her.

"Has the devil got you? That girl's busy. Every decent person's busy. But even if she wasn't, she wouldn't stop for the likes of you." She held her kerchief tight under her chin with one hand, and with the other she pointed a mud-caked finger at him. "Where'd you steal those clothes? Are there more, thief?"

"I'm Don Giovanni, old fool."

"Oh, Don Giovanni," she said in mock humility. "A visit from Don Giovanni. I'm not worthy of this honor."

"Your sarcasm is outrageous." Despite his indignant words, he realized the woman's impression made sense. If the girl had seen him, which he wasn't even sure of, she must have taken him for a ruffian in gentleman's clothes. He should go home and wash himself, rest his weary body. Every drop of energy drained away just like that. His spirit wept from exhaustion.

Don Giovanni walked back to his castle, eyes on the ground so he wouldn't see the faces of those who called for help. He was too tired to be of use.

It was evening when he got home. The servants were

nowhere around. Well, that was all right. They should have asked permission, it was true. But he would have given it. They were caring for their kinsfolk, no doubt.

He walked through the large hall where the party had taken place. No one had cleaned up.

When he was a child, his maidservant taught him strict rules about touching food. He always used the very tips of his fingers. And he dipped them afterward in a bowl of water that she would hold. Scented water: lemon in summer, clove in winter. He never licked his fingers. But in this moment he didn't even know where a clean bowl could be found. He stood by the table and ate, then licked his fingers clean. It felt oddly daring.

He stripped off his dirty clothes and kicked them into a pile. They were beyond help. He'd tell Betta to burn them. There was no one to bring him water for a scrubbing. But there were pitchers of wine on the table. He bathed in marsala, and slept in the haze of intoxication.

In the morning, he rang the bell for his personal manservant, Lino. No one came. He'd been abandoned. Who was going to take care of him?

That's exactly what he had wondered when he'd been told his parents were dead. But now the question was laughable. He had turned nineteen in December. He took care of himself when it came to everything important. As for the details of daily living, well, he could do without Lino for a day.

He dressed, ran a brush through his thick, curly hair, and went out to the table in the grand hall. He ate standing. Some foods had already turned rancid.

He started down the path toward the city, and came across a boy. "You're Lino's nephew, aren't you?"

The boy stared up at him blankly.

"Tell him to come back to work. And tell him to tell Betta to get all the servants to come back, too." His words sounded ridiculous, even to himself. He hadn't really thought them through. What if the servants' quarters had been ruined? "All that aren't needed elsewhere, that is." But even that addition rang shrill with absurdity. Every able hand was needed everywhere.

The boy stood there.

Was he trying to shame Don Giovanni? The insolent little snot-nose. "Well, go on," he said gruffly.

The boy ran off.

Don Giovanni continued along the path, through the city gate. He was sickened by the destruction. How on earth had he been so lucky as to have no damage from the wave? But wait, his sheep flocks habitually covered the lower part of the hillside between the castle and the beach. A thousandfold. No one had more sheep than Don Giovanni. He didn't use them for wool; Sicilian wool could never match the quality of imported wools. But they were important for cheese and meat. A solid source of income. He couldn't remember seeing any of them since the night he'd watched the woman walk into the sea.

He turned back and crossed the countryside to survey his lands. He walked up and down, back and forth, for hours. Bloated carcasses littered the hill. Not a single living ewe, a single living ram. Not one had had the sense to run to higher land.

Disease followed death, any fool knew that. All those carcasses needed to be gathered and burned. The sooner, the better.

Don Giovanni went back to the castle and stopped at the entrance. He rang the bell to call his servants.

He paced the front patio, making plans. Now and then he glanced out over the hillside, over the town. But the view upset him too much.

He rang the bell again.

What was keeping them? Surely the boy had delivered his message. Surely Lino had obeyed. Or someone else. There must have been someone who returned to work.

He rang again and again.

He went inside. A chill met him; the hearth fire had gone out. He walked the castle halls, entered every room, even the servants' quarters. With each room, his steps got faster, so that by the end he was running flat out. The place was empty. And not just empty, it was stripped. The draperies, the rugs, the furniture, gone. Everything had been taken in the hours that he'd been out on the hill.

"Thieves!" shouted Don Giovanni. He burst from the front

door and ran along the footpath, heart and feet thumping hard. He knew where Lino's family lived, didn't he? He'd heard once.

But when he got to the house, he didn't recognize anyone there. "Where's Lino?" he asked.

A woman made tsking noises at him, but a man pointed him along the road.

He knocked on a door. Lino opened it.

The stench came strong as a punch. Don Giovanni fell back a few steps. "Come," he said. "I need you."

Lino pointed. In a corner of the room a woman sat on the floor with a child limp across her legs. Her hands braided the dead girl's hair. Even with her face turned away, Don Giovanni could feel the madness in her eyes.

"I'm sorry," he said in a hushed voice. "Is that your wife and daughter?"

"My sister and niece."

"I'm so sorry." Don Giovanni's mind reeled in the face of such wrenching grief. What was he doing here? What could anyone do? God's will.

Nothing to be done.

Damnable, defeated thinking. There was always something to do, something to make right. He put his hands on his forehead to steady his brain. "Come with me, Lino. The sheep need to be burned. We have to catch thieves." He knew he sounded incoherent, Lino's face told him that, but an explanation would take too long. "Hurry!"

Lino shook his head.

Don Giovanni put his hands on the man's shoulders and squeezed. "Working helps. And you need to make a living."

"I can't make a living from you, sire."

"Of course you can. You're my personal servant."

Lino shook his head. "You have nothing to pay me with, sire."

"Don't be ridiculous. I'm wealthy."

"We all know the truth." Lino shut the door in Don Giovanni's face.

What could Lino have meant? What truth?

Don Giovanni went through parts of town he'd never been in, searching faces. Betta. He could ask where she lived, but there had to be many women named Betta. And everyone was busy. The frenetic activity of the day before, the digging through wreckage, the search for loved ones, all of that was over. Sorrows and losses consumed people now. Wailing rose on all sides. He couldn't ask anything; he didn't want to intrude on strangers.

His friends. They'd help, of course. He was already on the road to one's home; it didn't make sense to go back in the opposite direction to the castle for a horse. Besides, the brisk night air revived him. So he walked.

But that brief distance turned long, after all. He followed country roads, from noble to noble the whole evening. The story was always the same: everyone had suffered losses. Workers disappeared or injured. Flocks of sheep washed away. Crops destroyed by the saltwater. No one could help him—not now.

Their indifference shocked him. If the tables were turned, he would never have treated any of them so callously. What was going on?

Don Giovanni had no choice but to throw himself on the mercy of Don Alfinu. He was weary when he reached the old man's castle.

The servant Masu led him to Don Alfinu, who was just finishing his meal: a bowl of vermicelli with oil and garlic—a popular new dish—and a plate of raw sardine fillets under vinegar. The old man ate lightly, because he suffered from indigestion in the night. Don Giovanni remembered his belches and farts.

"Good evening, sire," said Don Giovanni, trying to keep his eyes off the food, which made his stomach clench. "I trust the wave left you without harm."

"Dispense with the formalities. You've come with something to say—you've said it to everyone else already. Don't think I don't know. But I get to speak first. Do you realize how much money I've lent you in the past year?"

Don Giovanni stared at the old man's mouth. A fleck of silver stuck to his bottom lip. Sardine skin. It looked delicious. How could he be this hungry? He licked his own lip. "None, sire."

"You brainless sot. I told you to keep a ledger."

"And I intend to. Soon."

Don Alfinu brought his open hand down on the table with a wham. "It's too late now. How many spectacles did you think you could host? You're not the king, you know. You're not a duke or even a prince. I told you to rein yourself in. I told you. But you went your own way, buying gifts for loose women, throwing party after party."

Did he really have to listen to this rant? Don Giovanni was tempted to leave. But he didn't know where to go. He spread his hands in reason. "Why count coins when there's an infinite number?"

"Blockhead! You spent them all. Your servants rely on me for pay while you throw money to the winds."

His servants had gone to Don Alfinu behind his back? "They should have told me. Lino, Betta, they should have."

"No one could tell you anything. You never listen. I figured I could get it back from your sheep if I had to. And now . . ." He flung his hands up. "The whole blasted lot of them dead. And I'm the one holding the bag."

Don Giovanni's head felt like a huge lump of clay on the weak stalk of his neck. He grasped the edge of the table for support. "I'll call in my loans. Everyone owes me money."

"After this wave, exactly who has extra money?"

Don Giovanni swallowed hard. "I'll pay you back."

"You don't need to."

Surprising words from a stingy man. "Thank you, but I'll repay you anyway."

"Look around."

Don Giovanni looked. Against the far wall was a cabinet he recognized as his mother's. Beside it was a table that his father had used for rolling out maps to study. "You're the thief?" he breathed, incredulous.

Don Alfinu laughed. "Don't be absurd." Exactly the maid-servant's words, before this nightmare began. "Your castle is now mine. I'll sell it. Ever since that old King Roger put a moratorium on building castles, they've been hard to come by. It will go high. We'll be even."

Everything gone. That's why his friends hadn't offered to help. They knew. His problem was so enormous, none could begin to help. "And what becomes of me?"

"You should have worried about that before. With that wave, your last hope at solvency washed away. You can go down to the kitchen now, and beg the cook for old bread and a bowl of sauce. And don't get fresh with her. A randy poor man has even less charm than a randy rich one.

"Let's hope you do a better job at a beggar's life than you did at a don's."

Thieves

THOUGH THE MOONLIGHT WAS EXCEPTIONALLY STRONG, DON Giovanni wouldn't rely on his eyes alone. They had to be wrong. He felt in every cupboard, every drawer.

Now he stood in the kitchen. The shelves were bare. He swept his hands along them a second time. Nothing.

This couldn't be.

Don Alfinu had no heart.

He slid to the floor and slept sitting. Or tried to. The noises of the night kept sneaking up and grabbing him by the throat. From outside the window thumps and a squeak cut off midway. An owl had caught a hare. Or perhaps it was a fox. From the pantry came scurrying, chirping, chirring. Dormice? A small plop, then the crack of an insect crushed in a gecko's jaw. The random groan of wood.

As dawn came, he gave up. He stretched his chill-stiffened limbs. In the haze he saw them hanging from a hook outside the door down to the empty wine cellar: three goatskin bags, overlooked or judged useless. When Don Giovanni went partridge hunting, Lino would fill a bag with watered red wine. Nothing refreshed better in midmorning.

Don Giovanni went to the well in the courtyard and pulled up a bucket. He filled the bags and slung them over his shoulder. He walked through the castle one last time. The ring of his footsteps in the empty rooms was almost eerie. Spots he'd played in as a boy felt unfamiliar. It was the starkness that did it. No texture. Texture was such a big part of recognition—life had lost texture.

He found a wool cap, dropped in haste. Nothing else. He'd never known servants to be so thorough.

He put on the cap and stared up at the painted dining hall ceiling. The light through the windows wasn't strong enough yet to illuminate that high up. He could barely make out the colors, much less the figures. Well, it didn't matter, for he knew every detail by heart. Women half clad offering food to eager men, with musicians in the background. It wasn't the figures that he'd seen there as a boy. After his parents died, Don Alfinu had had the ceiling repainted with war scenes and angels. But when Don Giovanni had taken over the castle again, he paid the finest artists to bring the ceiling back to the spirit his parents had intended. Actually, to a spirit even more sensual than the original. Homage to the good things in life, the things he was born and bred to enjoy.

He gritted his teeth. Nothing made sense. What was he to do next?

Slap.

Footsteps in the entrance hall. Bare ones. And without a voice announcing them. The nerve.

Don Giovanni strode across the room. "Who's there?"

No answer.

He ran to the entrance hall.

Two men stood by the open door, ready to flee. Peasants, by their clothes.

"What do you mean, coming in unbidden like this?"

"Your Excellency," said the younger man with a slight bow, but not backing up. "We heard it was abandoned."

"Abandoned," echoed the other. His eyes were taking in the bare walls and floors. He craned his neck like a vulture to see into the room behind Don Giovanni.

Don Giovanni moved to the side to break his line of sight. "You heard wrong."

"No horses in the pasture." The man shrugged. "Nor the stable."

No horses. The breath went out of him as fast as if he'd been punched in the gut. Don Giovanni hadn't checked the stable. No horses. He had to force himself to reason. Logic told him it was just as well. If the horses had been cooped up in the stable, they'd have suffered, for he hadn't thought to feed or water them. He hoped the donkeys were gone, too.

The younger man put out his hand. "Anything you can spare, sire." His arm was skinny; his hand, bony.

"A little charity." The other extended his claw.

Neither wore a jacket on this cold morning.

Don Giovanni looked at the open palms. That's what he would be reduced to if he didn't come up with a plan fast. He held his own hands out. His pale, soft hands beside their brown, rough ones. Laughter bubbled up. Lack of sleep on top of everything else was making him hysterical, but he couldn't afford to give in to it. He couldn't afford anything. He pressed a hand over his mouth to hold in the laugh at that joke.

The younger man cocked his head. "You don't look well, sire. Do you even know about the disaster?"

"The wave, sire," said the other man. "Came and smashed everything. Washed people clear away. Don't you know?" He spoke as though to an idiot.

Don Giovanni had always given to the less fortunate. Always. His father said Muslims had that rule right, a foundation for a superior civilization; it was built into their religion—give to the poor. Give. Give, give, give to the poor. "I have nothing to give."

"Fine clothes, and nothing to give?"

"I don't owe you an explanation." Don Giovanni straightened his collar. Humiliations lay ahead; he didn't need to start early. "You're trespassing."

"And whose property would it be, sire?" asked the other man. "Yours?"

"Or are you trespassing, too?" asked the younger man. He cozied up beside Don Giovanni as if in cahoots.

Insufferable! "I was born here. I'm Don Giovanni."

"Oh, Don Giovanni takes the time to speak to us," said the other man. "I'm not worthy of this honor."

The words the old crone had said. Words that almost always meant the opposite of what the speaker was thinking. Don Giovanni waved them away.

"What's in those bags?" asked the younger man.

"Get out of here." Don Giovanni was too tired to deal with this nonsense. He walked toward the door.

The younger man blocked his way. "How about a wager? You're an educated man, the way you talk. You probably read massive tomes all the time. In funny languages, too, right? But I bet I can tell you a truth you've never thought about before, excellent scholar."

Could this possibly get more vexing? "Of course you can. You work in your world, I work in mine. We know different things." Don Giovanni tried to walk around him.

The man jumped in his path again. "A truth about human nature." He held one finger up in front of Don Giovanni's eyes. "If I can tell you a truth about human nature, one you never thought about before, I get those goatskin bags. Deal?"

"I don't gamble."

"You hear that?" the younger man said to the other. "He's a godless man."

Of all the ridiculous things. Don Giovanni raised his voice. "How would you know the first thing about me?"

"It takes hope to gamble. And a man without hope is a man without God." The younger man smiled and held out his hand.

Don Giovanni shook his head.

"I told you a truth you hadn't thought about before."

"I didn't accept the wager." Don Giovanni pushed the man aside and walked through the door. He squinted in the rude sunlight. Which way to turn? Did it matter?

He took a step when—*whap!*—he went sprawling. Pain bloomed between the wings of his shoulders. It billowed down his spine, up his neck. He curled one arm backward to reach the source of the searing heat.

Crack! His hand diverted quickly to the back of his head, where it hurt much worse than his shoulders. The wool hat was sticky wet.

"Serves you right."

The breath that delivered those words hit Don Giovanni warm in his face. The young man was squatting beside him, his cheeks dark with anger. And that breath so foul, Don Giovanni stopped his own breathing in order to be free of it. He closed his eyes.

"If you'd have paid up, we three could have had a bag each. But you showed no mercy. You get what you give."

Don Giovanni felt the goatskin bags ripped from his shoulder. He felt the shoes pulled from his feet.

"Another truth," came the stink, close again now. "The world's gone bad out there. Commit that to memory."

He felt tugs on his trousers.

"Leave him his trousers, at least," said the voice of the other man.

"We can sell them."

His trousers were jerked from his legs.

Don Giovanni passed out.

When he finally opened his eyes, the sun's glare made him close them again fast. His eyes hurt, his head hurt, his back hurt. And he was cold. It was still full daylight—so he must not have been unconscious that long. He sat up slowly, fighting off dizziness. All that remained to his name was the shirt he wore, blood spattered on the left shoulder, and the wool cap.

He carefully peeled the cap off. His hair was a mat of congealed blood. It hurt just to smooth it.

Now that the weight of his head wasn't pressing it down against the ground, his bottom lip hurt, too. His teeth had cut the inside when he fell. He used the clean cap edge to wipe the dirt off. He tossed the cap away.

He stood. Surprisingly, he wasn't shaky. He must not have lost as much blood as he'd thought.

He took off his shirt and tied it around his waist, like an apron. It covered his private parts. He would go to a friend's home. They'd give him clothes. And food. It was simple charity.

Only then someone else would just rob him again. Nobles' clothes wouldn't serve him in his role as beggar. The role Don Alfinu had cast him in.

Well, not everyone destitute was a beggar. He could work. Peasants did. He'd start by going back to Lino's.

He rubbed his arms and chest and moved quickly. The rocks of the path cut his tender feet.

Women dressed in the black of mourning passed and looked the other way, embarrassed for him. Children pointed at his backside and laughed. Men in black looked through him; he didn't exist.

All of them had nothing. Less than nothing—they had the misery of the wave, the reasons for the black clothes. Yet they felt superior. Because of his bare bottom.

This was a nightmare. He was Don Giovanni. The richest baron around. The most handsome bachelor of Messina. People looked with admiration when he passed. This wasn't happening. This couldn't be happening.

But each step of his bare feet proved it was.

He veered around the dead fish and seaweed, broken dishes and benches washed from people's homes, drowned cats, dogs, even birds. And a lone deer, a stupid thing that had strayed from the forest at exactly the wrong time.

Given the rate he was going and the breeze that had picked up, he was a quivering mass of gooseflesh by the time he finally stood in front of Lino's door. He knocked.

A sharp-nosed woman came out of the next house.

He wiped his hair off his face and nodded politely.

She spat on the ground, as though he were a bearer of ill fortune. Her suspicious mug reminded him of the old crone who'd called him a thief the morning before.

He rapped harder on Lino's door. When no one answered, he went in. The odor of death hovered over the empty room. He called out just to be sure. Then he sank onto the bench by the table to wait.

It would be safe to sleep here. Heaven knew his body needed the rest. But his eyes roved the room. There were clothes in the basket in the corner. He knew, because the stiff, wide weave of the wicker allowed a glimpse inside.

On a shelf was the end of a round of bread. The smell of it fought with the odor of death. His mouth watered.

Don Giovanni was no thief.

On the other hand, he'd been generous with Lino. In the year that Lino had been in his employ, he must have been generous many times. He couldn't remember now. He remembered gifts to his friends, though, so surely he must have done similar things for Lino. What? Just one thing—that's all he needed to ease the guilt already rising in his chest. But nothing came to mind. His head wasn't functioning properly after that blow. There had to have been many acts of generosity. Many.

He folded his arms across his bare chest and hugged himself. He could wait.

But his eyes prowled now. Sneaky. They returned to the basket of clothes, the bread on the shelf.

That jug under the shelf probably held wine.

Don Giovanni walked over and opened it. The floral aroma of Malvasia made him giddy. He would have preferred something not so sweet, but then, beggars can't be choosers. He laughed at his joke and took a long drink.

He dumped out the basket. A woman's dress. It draped from his hands like a maid in full surrender. Long sleeves, long skirts, guardians of modesty. And a girl's dress. Such a simple thing, a swathe of cloth to hide the body that would one day lure. A man's smock and pants. What weak things humans used to protect against the forces.

This was all they had—the clothes on their back and one extra set. His cheeks went slack. A meager life.

But his fingers tightened around the trousers and smock. It was regrettable, but unavoidable. With all the dead in Messina now, it shouldn't be hard to find another outfit. Don Giovanni needed these clothes immediately, whereas Lino already had some. Lino had the luxury of time to get replacements from the dead.

Don Giovanni winced as he pulled the smock fast over his cut head. The coarse cloth scratched his skin. He donned the trousers just as quickly. After all, once the decision was made, hesitation was pointless. Dangerous, even. What if Lino came home and objected? The thought of such a mortifying scene turned Don Giovanni's stomach. He grabbed the bread and walked out the door, chewing at it.

"Thief!" screamed the old woman from her post next door. "I knew it." She held out a dried hot red pepper toward him, a talisman against evil. "Thief! Thief!"

Don Giovanni ran. With every third step, it seemed a rock jabbed his tender soles. He looked over his shoulder.

Four little boys had taken chase.

He twirled to face them, holding his arms up and out. "Don't be foolish," he said firmly. "Go back home."

The boys stopped and closed ranks; eight black eyes burned at him. Barefoot and filthy, the lot.

The sharp-nosed hag caught up to the boys. Her arms were clasped around a basket of bashed and stinking fish. Another woman came running up. "Quick," the women said to the boys. "Quick, quick."

Instantly, Don Giovanni understood what was about to happen. He turned and ran, despite his wounded feet.

Rotted fish parts came hurtling onto his back.

"Thief!" screamed the chorus. "Thief!"

The Forest

THE STONES OF THE HILL PATH WERE LOOSE AND DON GIOVANNI moved fast. Too fast. He fell into thistles with needles longer than his nose. He rolled away, slapping hard at the flaming sting in his feet, ankles, calves. How hideous to have no shoes.

He rocked from side to side and screamed in pain. Squirrels chattered back at him. Nightingales, warblers, buntings sprang to attention, watched beadily, then resumed their singing. Spring was coming, they insisted. Spring, food, sex. The splendor of it only drove Don Giovanni to tears of frustration.

He uncurled himself with difficulty. He stood and surveyed the path. The rocks looked loose for as far as he could see. There was no choice but to go through the forests, dense with birch and holm oak and undergrowth that poked and pricked. That was better than thistles, though.

He ate the last of the bread. Then he balled his hands into fists against the pain and walked and walked. Finally he stumbled across a beech grove, with its characteristic ground cover of fungus and moss. A respite for his poor feet, at last. He collapsed.

When he woke, he pushed his back up against a smooth trunk and stroked his feet and ankles. The flame was gone, but it was as though the memory of it lingered in his limbs. His skin hurt just at this light touch.

He walked on. The sunlight played off yellow flowers on spindly stems. Orchids? His mother used to pay great sums for orchids from the slopes of Etna. What a surprise to find them here. With the sun on them, the ground seemed stippled with gold. An altar.

His mouth was dry. He needed food, but first, water. He hiked northward fast, despite the rocks and sticks. It was full afternoon; only a few hours of light left. Hurry.

Soon he reached the shore of the long, narrow Ganzirri Lake, with its whitish-blue water. Bee-eaters, fabulous in their green throats and yellow and orange chests, sent rolling trills from the sandy banks. Purple martins flitted past. Slender-billed gulls cried out. Near the opposite bank flamingoes fed. Behind them the mountains held deep grooves hollowed out by the streams of torrential spring rains. The rocks alternated stripes of gray and darker gray, like the folds of a woman's skirt, now catching the light, now falling into shadow. Don Giovanni gaped. Such extreme natural beauty demanded attention even now, in his terrible straits.

He pulled his smock off, careful of his wounds, and spread it neatly in the sun. The same with his trousers. This way they'd absorb whatever warmth the sun offered and they'd feel so much better when he put them back on.

He slipped into the water. Cold, but hardly more than the air. This was a marine lake, connected to the sea by two channels, no good for drinking. But salt made wounds heal; swimming was medicine for his feet and head.

The waters teemed with anchovies, eels, bass, mullet. If only he had a way to catch them.

He came out on the mountainside and went straight to the natural spring, where warm water thick with minerals bubbled up through the rocks into a little pool. He drank until his belly was a swollen melon.

He sat in the warm water, legs folded, and rested his forehead against a rock. What next? Without a home the elements affected you much more. The sun. The rain.

As a child, Don Giovanni had listened to the servants talk. They believed you could predict weather from the gassiness of this thermal spring. Extra gassy meant rain would come. It seemed very gassy, yet the sky was clear.

The faintest breeze came, carrying the pungent perfume of rosemary. His stomach contracted, but he wasn't up to chewing those needles in the wild. People said fairies inhabited rosemary, wicked fairies that shape-shifted into snakes. He didn't believe that, of course. Nevertheless . . .

He walked back around the tip of the lake and dressed slowly. He ached everywhere. Someone simply had to help him. Someone had to put a stop to this awfulness.

Who was he kidding? His best friends hadn't offered anything. Not even the truth; they'd let him go to Don Alfinu's unaware, easy prey for the old man's malice.

The words of the thief this morning came back: *The world's gone bad out there.* Had an inconsequential thief who fancied himself a philosopher made Don Giovanni lose confidence in humanity just like that?

He wandered, racking his brains for a plan.

Dusk made the woods dreamlike. Yellow fluttered in his peripheral vision. It gave the odd sensation that he was fluttering, too—floating on the breath of the woods.

Don Giovanni walked softly toward where the yellow cloud had passed. A group of almond trees with their clusters of small pink blossoms had attracted butterflies. It was early for almonds; usually their budding coincided with the start of Lent. The trees hadn't even leafed out yet. Blossoms on bare branches. And so many butterflies all over them. Lemon-colored. Like the butterflies he'd seen the morning his parents died.

That sense of being before an altar returned. Maybe it was the effect of having gone so long without food.

On the ground in little clumps among the trees were

pendulous snowdrops. Bees crawled inside the white bells. Bees in your garden were auspicious. They meant prosperity was on the way. He walked toward them.

Trotting came from behind. He knew without looking there was no chance of outrunning it. He dived behind a tree.

The black-brown boar raced after him. Around and around the tree. He was small, barely up to Don Giovanni's thigh, but his tusks extended upward a hand's length. They could slash the life out of a man. Danger, danger, danger beat the drum of Don Giovanni's running feet.

Until he fell.

In an instant, the boar stood over him. It straddled his arm. It huffed and puffed, tense and strong.

Was Don Giovanni's arm long enough to grab this boar's scrotum? He slowly stretched it, at the ready.

Man and beast waited. A standoff.

Somehow the boar gave in first. Or maybe the animal just lost interest. He wandered over to the snowdrops and ate flowers and bees together indiscriminately. Then he rutted in the roots of the tree.

Don Giovanni breathed shallowly. If the boar didn't hear or smell him, it might forget him. Already it was far enough away that it probably couldn't see him well; boars were notoriously poor-sighted. Finally, the animal trotted off.

Don Giovanni lay in the dirt unmoving. Slowly the tension

left. He felt heavy, so heavy he might never be able to get up. He might blend into the earth.

Somewhere in the back of his brain he realized he had entertained the idea that he could live in the forest temporarily. That way he wouldn't have to demean himself by begging. That idea had now been exposed as absurd.

He got to his feet. He would sleep on a beach tonight. Tomorrow he would walk south, past Messina. He'd never seek peasants' work where people might recognize him. But there were other cities.

At last, a plan.

Water

THE RAIN PELTED HIM. EVEN WITH BOTH ARMS CURLED around his head, even bone-tired, Don Giovanni couldn't sleep. It wasn't that the rain was cold; no, the weather had turned decidedly springlike. It was the driving force of it. It beat him numb.

He gave up, got to his feet, and walked.

It would be delightful to be in a home right now. Homes slowed you down, calmed your innards, smoothed you out. Homes rested the skin and the eyes and the heart.

The absence of home was Hell. Don Giovanni had been thinking about the ancient Greeks, and he'd decided Hades was a better picture of the afterlife than Hell. Hades had a river—fresh water free for the taking anytime—and dark corners offering shelter and shade. Hell, in contrast, was aflame and wide open.

Don Giovanni had never questioned his Catholicism before. The philosopher-thief back at his castle called him godless for not being willing to gamble. It was true that gambling took hope and hope was necessary for faith. But the converse didn't hold: a nongambler could have both faith and hope. Don Giovanni enjoyed easy pleasures—good food, good women. Gambling wasn't easy; you might lose, and if you won, someone else lost. So his avoidance of wagers, dice games, and lotteries added up to an avoidance of unpleasantness, not a lacking in his spiritual self.

No, he hadn't ever questioned his Catholicism. No educated Sicilian took paganism seriously, not in these modern times. Right now he was just sick of being exposed to the elements.

The beach sand turned grainy with the rain. It scratched his cut feet. He hobbled to the water and waded in up to his knees. The salt stung, but the sand on the bottom changed to silk here, caressing, like a fine woman's gown or, better, like her thighs.

A fishing boat came into sight. Two men rowed, side by side, one oar each. They waved.

Don Giovanni waved back. Fishing was better in the rain, but this was a downpour. Crazy men.

He waded back to the water's edge and sat. The waves sloshed around his trouser legs. The rain gradually let up. He dug his fingers into the wet sand at his sides and pulled up *cannolicchie*—razor shell clams—and dropped them in his lap. When he had a big pile, he took the largest and squeezed hard on one end. The white flesh squished out the other end. He bit it and jerked his head back, pulling the animal from the shell.

He'd been feeding on these clams the three days it took to walk here. But they couldn't keep a man alive indefinitely. Bread was necessary. Meat now and then. Fruits, beans, greens.

So, while he avoided towns, he went into the small, scattered homes along the way to ask for water and exchange his services for food. Everyone gave water. But when it came to food, a stingier bunch of folk he'd never seen before. The way they acted, you'd think a crust of bread was a leg of lamb. And a dried fig, well, that was nothing less than a king's banquet. Even oranges were hard to come by unless he sneaked into an orchard.

Once he met a man with a cart of goods for sale along a back road. The nervous vendor asked him to stand by the cart to protect it from thieves and to keep his donkey from running off while he defecated in a field. In payment all Don Giovanni had been allowed was to suck dregs from the bottom of the man's lunch bowl. Chewed, spit-out gristle.

Better to eat clams. So he returned to the beaches.

He sighed. Maybe he'd sleep now. He preferred to walk through the night, letting the heat of exertion warm him, and sleep in the day, when the sunlight warmed him.

"Hello, there."

Don Giovanni opened his eyes and squinted against the resplendent sun. The fishermen had rowed to shore and one of them stood in the water at his feet, holding the boat by a rope. The other sat in the boat watching. He tipped his head.

"Do you have your wits about you?"

Don Giovanni shrugged.

"Can you row?"

Don Giovanni could use work. But the very thought of being on the water in that tiny boat all day made him seasick. "Truth be told, I despise the idea."

The man jerked his head. "You talk funny. Fancy."

"Everyone tells me that."

"We're in need, what with the quake making so much trouble in Taormina. Can't you help a while?"

"Taormina felt the quake then, too? Did you get a gigantic wave?"

"No. The quake was enough."

Don Giovanni smoothed the new beard forming on his chin. "I guess I'll circle around Taormina, then, and head straight for Catania."

The man pushed out his lips. "That's a mistake."

"What do you mean?"

"It started with Etna. The largest crater erupted and the cone side that faces Taormina fell—disappeared down the crater. *Boom!*" He made an arc in the air with his free arm. "My cousin was awake. He saw it. The quake that followed destroyed Catania." He thrust his face toward Don Giovanni and grimaced. "Thousands killed."

"It couldn't be that many," said Don Giovanni. "Catania's only a third the size of Messina."

"Oh, it was thousands, all right. It happened on the vigil of the Feast of Saint Agata. And her being the patron saint who guards against earthquakes." He tilted his head and moved forward. "But she didn't guard this time. People came to the cathedral from everywhere for the celebration. Benedictine monks. Bishops, too. The bishop that carried the veil from Saint Agata's tomb that's supposed to protect against earthquakes, even he was killed." He nodded. "Thousands dead. You'd be out of your mind to go there now."

"Thanks for the information." Don Giovanni rinsed the sand from the seat of his pants. He walked up to the road.

His lips had gone cold at the mention of the Feast of Saint Agata. His ears buzzed. He felt almost drunk. Maybe some of the clams he'd eaten had been bad. He walked fast, to try to shake off this sensation.

It wasn't long before a cart came. A dark cloth covered the high load. The driver tugged at his wide hat brim and sat up tall as he passed. He waved over a shoulder without looking back. His hanging feet bounced in the air with the donkey's trot. The road went uphill and down; the cart slowed on the up and sped on the down.

Don Giovanni liked vendors' carts. The wheels stood chest high. The dozen spokes were arm length. Perched above the axle was a wooden box no longer than the diameter of the wheels, with a bench seat for the driver. The effect was comical. It lifted his spirits. And the side decorations were in vivid paints: cathedrals and battle scenes. He ran behind it.

The cart reached the crossroads and turned left, toward Taormina. Don Giovanni went right. Inland. Toward the northern slopes of Mount Etna. Randazzo was his new goal.

To the south he looked out over the Alcantara Gorge, with the river running through. Spectacular. The rock formation was the result of Mount Etna. The shape of everything around here was the result of the Mountain.

The road went steadily uphill. The rare houses were one story with wooden roofs. It made sense; people here lived in dread of quakes that could bring a roof crashing down in seconds. Stone roofs were caskets in disguise.

A shrill call drew his attention to a small lake. In the sky over it were two flashes of brilliant blue. Now he saw orange. Kingfishers. One was diving, but the other kept landing on his back. They tumbled in the air, spinning blue and orange. The attacker grabbed the other by his bill and held him underwater. Then he flew off.

Don Giovanni waited. The other bird didn't resurface.

Coots swam happily near shore, pumping their heads. Mallards glided on fat breasts, undisturbed by the recent drama. In two months there would be nests to raid. But nothing now. No fruits on trees. No berries on bushes. The only way to get food now was to stage another drama.

He took off his smock and filled it with stones from the side of the road. Then he walked down to the lake. He piled the stones on the shore and put on his smock. He folded each hand around a stone.

The mallards took directly to the air. The coots dove and resurfaced far away. He knew they would.

He sat quiet and still. The ducks would return.

A hen mallard came first. Then another. Then several. They dabbled happily. Closer. Closer.

Don Giovanni threw the stones. He picked up more and threw harder. The flock rose in a frenzy of quacks. When they were gone, a drake lay struggling on the water.

Don Giovanni waded in and broke the duck's neck. He gashed through feathers and skin with the edge of a stone. He ripped the flesh with his teeth. He had eaten many things raw, but never birds. The taste wasn't bad, though. The blood was hot and salty. The meat was dark and rich.

He ate the liver, kidneys, gizzard, brain, eyes, tongue. He drank lake water and rinsed himself. It was important to stay clean, to look as good as possible.

His trousers were wet, and the air here was distinctly cooler than down near the shore. At this altitude the broom plants and other shrubs were plentiful, but they offered little protection from the wind. He spied a pine grove uphill. He ran, clutching his chest, rubbing his forearms. His teeth chattered.

The floor of the grove was thick with needles. He took off

his wet clothes, spread them on the ground, then sprinkled the aromatic needles over them, to cover any scent that might remain from the duck meal. Wildcats were more abundant here than up near Messina.

He tunneled his way deep under the needles; they formed a layer over him, his clothes being a second layer, and the top needles a third. Only his nose protruded.

His body warmed, but his lips were still cold. They'd been cold since the fisherman had mentioned Saint Agata. Why?

Now Don Giovanni remembered: the name of the maidservant who had been rude the night of the wave, the name that wouldn't come to his tongue before, was Agata.

Mountain Life

DON GIOVANNI WAS UNABLE TO SEE HIS OWN BODY IN THE thick mountain fog. A hint of horror crept across his skin; Messina hardly ever had fog. He dressed quickly, chewed several small crustaceans that crackled in his teeth, and hiked out to the road. It was barely dawn.

As he walked, he went over everything he knew about Saint Agata. The way to dispel foolishness was to beat it down with reason. Curses were pagan foolishness. Once when he was little, a nursemaid had strung garlic around his neck to protect against the evil eye. His mother had ripped it off with a laugh and roasted the garlic as a spread for flat bread.

Saint Agata was born in Catania, right? Or was it Palermo? Either way, she was buried in Catania. Almost a thousand years ago. She was rich. Gorgeous. A Christian at a time when pagan

Romans ruled Sicily. She was to be executed for her faith, but a magistrate tried to force her to his bed in exchange for not arresting her. She refused, was thrown in prison, beaten. Her beautiful breasts were amputated. She was rolled on burning coals. But before she died, an earthquake struck and killed her tormentors.

The magistrate managed to get away, though.

A martyred virgin. Saint Agnes of Rome had a similar fate, but she was beheaded, instead. Saint Apollonia of Alexandria had her teeth bashed in before she was burned alive. The list went on and on.

But none of this had anything to do with Don Giovanni. That maidservant couldn't have been Saint Agata in disguise. She carried an ordinary platter of ordinary food, not a silver one holding severed breasts. She wore brown cotton, not white linen. And, most of all, Saint Agata would never bother Don Giovanni, for he had never mistreated a maiden. He took only what was freely offered, and then with appreciation and gratitude.

No virgin saint had any business cursing him, even if he did believe in curses, which he didn't. All the wretched things that had befallen him had simply happened. Randomly. Rotten luck.

The fog burned off, allowing a view of the hills. The road wound through wide swaths of burned ground, where only the occasional stunted broom grew. Etna's wrath.

Just when Don Giovanni thought the world had turned barren, a stretch of rich dirt covered with yellow aconite blooms regaled his senses. Yellow again. Mere coincidence.

A cart passed. Two men on the driver's bench, and three boys in the cart, all pulled by one little donkey. Amazing. Five more children ran beside the cart. Who got to ride? Who had to run? Who meted out the justice?

Don Giovanni watched them roll out of sight. They waved once they were past, without looking back, like the man in the last cart. An hour's walk later Don Giovanni saw the children sitting in a circle in front of a small stone house with a steep wooden roof. In the middle of the circle was a tall, crude basket. They were working on something, but he couldn't see what.

They didn't wave this time, though he was sure they knew he watched. Mountain people were funny that way. They distrusted strangers. Not just Jews and Muslims—anyone not Greek. Charms hung around their necks.

A woman came out of the house. She swept ashes off the step, then went back inside. Mount Etna was easy to see from here. It spewed smoke, its constant state. A stretch of black forest—sticks, really—went off into the distance. The Mountain breathed dark clouds above it. The fetid smell touched everything.

Don Giovanni walked until the sun waned, and beyond. He made out red threads around one of the craters—small lava flows. With dusk he saw sparks.

It was much colder now, and still there were pockets of wildflowers: daisies, marigolds, sweet alyssum, pink-tipped asters, dandelions, crimson sorrel, violets. Mint and thyme and wild onion scented the air. How could they all grow when the earth was so cold?

Now and then he saw an isolated scattering of black pumice, as though the sky had rained rocks.

Don Giovanni's feet had hurt before, but now they were going numb. Still he tramped on.

It was the middle of the night when he reached the city walls. The gate creaked open with a heave of his shoulder. The town spread like a black-on-black painting. Nothing but looming shapes.

He turned up the first alley off the main road. An outside staircase on the corner building offered shelter underneath. He tucked his hands in his armpits, curled on his side into a tight ball, and willed himself not to flinch at the bark of the frantic dog that ran up and down beside him. The dog was tall and so thin, his ribs showed. But he was clearly frightened. So long as his barks didn't turn to growls, Don Giovanni would be all right. He slept.

A groan in his ear woke him. Don Giovanni opened one eye. A body pressed against him from behind. Warm. Part of it rested on his head. Bones weighed on his upper cheek. Another groan. And a bad smell.

He didn't dare move, but he opened his other eye now.

On the main road a goatherd drove his flock past. He wore trousers and a sheepskin coat. The animals moved in a cloud of hot breath. They'd be going out the town gate, to graze on dried tufts and those tricky wildflowers. Minutes later another flock passed. Then a third.

A boy in a dark blue cape that came down below his knees walked up the alley past Don Giovanni's staircase. He led four nannies on loose ropes. Their heavy udders swung blue-white in the cold. Neither boy nor goats looked at Don Giovanni.

The groan in Don Giovanni's ear turned to a whimper. The body behind him moved against his shoulders, pressing harder. Whiskers scratched his cheeks. Whiskers?

The goat boy stopped by the house door. He clanged on the iron wedge in his left hand.

A woman came out with a jug. The boy tucked the ends of his cape into his trousers. He squatted and milked a nanny right into the jug spout. The edgy smell brought tears of hunger to Don Giovanni's eyes. As the woman turned to go in, the boy pointed at Don Giovanni and left.

The woman put down the jug and picked up a rock by the side of the doorway. The way she did it, so fast, maybe she kept it there just for that. She held it in both hands and walked toward him. "Are you fairy or beggar?"

"Woof."

The weight lifted off Don Giovanni's cheek. The barker from the night before stepped over him and crouched at the woman's feet. He whined.

Don Giovanni sat up. He picked crust from his cheek.

Half-frozen dog drool. He clawed dog fur out of his thin beard. He smoothed his hair with both hands. He rubbed his teeth. Looking civilized had become elusive. Would a mirror shock him?

He wanted to stretch and straighten his smock and trousers, but he was afraid his height might spook the woman. Anyone who talked about fairies had to be skittish.

"Answer."

The dog sniffed at the milk jug. The woman kicked him away. With a yelp, the beast retreated across the alley.

"Answer," she hissed, coming toward him again.

When Don Giovanni was a child, his mother scolded him whenever he'd mimic a servant's talk. She said language was the clothing of the soul. How he dressed his ideas and aspirations played a role in how well they'd be received by others. And how well they were received by others played a role in how rich he could become. But oh, if only he could say just a few words exactly like this woman, coarse words to make her see him as a friend.

He shook his head.

"Don't you talk?"

He shrugged.

"Stand up."

Don Giovanni crawled from under the stairs and stood.

"Don't move." The woman held the rock at the ready. Skittish she wasn't. She turned her head and looked at him out of the corner of her eye. "If you tried to ride a grasshopper, you'd crush him." She raised one eyebrow slyly. "But then, not all fairies are small. You could belong to one of them new sects that mix with humans." She lowered her chin and looked up at him oddly. "You enchanted that mangy dog, after all. You could be a fairy." She thrust her chin forward fast. "Are you?"

Don Giovanni shook his head vehemently.

"I didn't think so, actually. You don't give off a glow, no matter how I look at you. A beggar, then?"

Don Giovanni shook his head.

She pursed her lips. "I could be kind to a beggar."

He hated that label. He shut his eyes. They burned under his trembling eyelids. The woman had goat milk.

He opened his eyes. His hands hung heavy at his sides, not turned palms up in the beggar's stance. His lips silent, not asking. But his eyes, oh, he couldn't keep his eyes from pleading. To silence them, he had only to close them again. He hated himself for not closing them.

"You're not bad-looking. And you're wiry. Strong." The woman blinked. "Wait." She went inside with the jug. She came out moments later and handed him a bowl of stale bread floating in steaming goat milk.

No spoon. How awful to use his fingers in front of a stranger. But she kept watching. At last he couldn't bear it anymore. He pushed the bread chunks under until they were soaked through and through, and he ate. Then he licked his fingers. He couldn't stop himself. He licked the bowl.

She took it back. "Wait here." Again she went into the house and returned quickly. This time she held shoes in one hand and a cape draped across her arm. The other hand was behind her back.

The shoes were of some sort of skin. They tied around Don Giovanni's feet snugly. The cape was coarse wool, dyed deep blue, like the one the goat boy wore. He put it on.

The woman considered him a moment. She took her other hand from behind her back and held out a large cloth bag.

Don Giovanni reached for it.

She pulled back. "Do well and there'll be more tasks."

That's what he'd hoped. He wanted to work, not beg.

"Fill this with snow. Bring it back by evening meal."

Snow? There was no snow other than on Etna.

She tapped her foot. "The work's hard, but it's all you'll get. Plenty of others want the easier jobs." She shook the bag. "And don't even think of running off with those clothes. Everyone in this part of town knows my master. And if you go into the German Lombard quarter, you'll get driven out. They hate beggars. And if you brave the Greek quarter, someone will steal that cape. Trousers and smock, too. No, you have no hope except here, in the Latin quarter. So you can't hide." She swung the bag. "Besides, my master would take it out on me if you made off with these. A pretty-faced lad like you wouldn't want to make a lass suffer, right?" Her face was sincere. She was taking a chance on him. A woman of faith.

He took the bag.

"Skim off the ashes before you scoop the snow." She went to the doorway, then turned. "Well, don't just stand there. You know where the Mountain is. Get moving."

So each day for the next month, Don Giovanni filled a bag with snow. The family he worked for supplied the rich of Randazzo with an evening dessert of sugared snow.

It was a strange town. Black even in full sun. The streets were paved with lava. Lava highlighted arches over doorways. All of Randazzo was a shrine to the volcano.

Everyone said the ground under Randazzo was blessed. Etna erupted often, destroying whole towns in a matter of hours. Neighboring villages came and went. In contrast, lava never entered Randazzo. Only ashes fell here; everyone swept their steps in the morning. Everyone wore hats and shook them off before entering buildings. They brushed off their cloaks. They stamped their boots. But those ashes were never from burned Randazzo homes. The town was blessed.

Don Giovanni didn't enter into talk about blessings. He listened carefully, though, whenever he was privy to talk—which wasn't often. After all, the lonely trek to find snow filled most of his day. Still, gradually he learned to mimic the tongue of the poorer people in the Latin quarter.

Soon he dared to open his mouth to ask for work from others. It was only fair; he'd served that one family for a month—so he'd earned those shoes and cape. More than earned them, actually. Don Giovanni had learned that few were willing to ascend the Mountain now because it wasn't frozen hard enough to offer sure footing anymore. The maidservant had taken advantage of his ignorance.

He took a perverse pride in knowing he'd braved such danger, and the spectacular view from the upper slopes struck awe into his heart every time. But the cold burned his hands. The sulfur in the air closest to the craters burned his eyes. The isolation burned his spirit.

As the weather warmed, work got easy to find. He ran errands, transported things around town, mucked out stables—anything in exchange for meals and a place to sleep.

The ground floors of the buildings were stables. Servants slept with donkeys, horses, goats. One flight up were stores and homes. Don Giovanni lay in a stall at night listening to rich people walk around overhead, living the life he was born to have.

He worked for anybody—in any quarter. But people could be nasty. They'd pick about the way he stacked the wood or the shape of a hole he'd dug. Anything to say he didn't deserve as much as they'd promised.

So soon he stopped that work. He became a champion eel catcher. He hunted at night, so he could watch stars while he waited. The river ran too fast in early spring for nets. So he learned how to make a trap—a *tarusi.* Eels entered into one chamber, passed to another, and couldn't turn around to get out again. Crabs were the best bait, and easy to get—they came after anything dead. So Don Giovanni picked rats off the town ratcatcher's pile.

Everyone ate eels, especially Catholics during Lent. Even after Easter they ate eels on Friday and Saturday, the no-meat days. Don Giovanni ate them, too.

Toward the middle of April rivers slowed and he caught elvers off the bank with his hands. Slippery, tickly.

By May the waters warmed with the air and the eels moved faster. They got harder to hold on to as he took them out of the trap. He switched to hunting frogs; the nights were loud with their chorus. He snipped off the heads and feet and peeled off the skin. Then he gutted them. A peasant boy taught him a trick: break the legs and they swell up and look plump, especially if you soak them in water. Don Giovanni had the plumpest frog legs of anyone. He could trade them to a tavern owner for a lamb dinner.

He caught snails by following the shiny slime on the ground after a rainfall. People loved them in sauces, especially the tiny ones with the transparent shells. He collected mountain fennel; it smelled stronger than the lowland herb—cooks gave him better treats in return.

The days were hot now, the nights balmy. Don Giovanni took to sleeping outdoors in the scent of mimosa, near goatherds. They told stories about the wilderness and he told stories about the sea. They had never seen the sea. No one they knew had traveled beyond Etna's slopes. They were agog at stories of squid and octopus, huge tuna and swordfish—and lobsters, they could hardly believe lobsters. Don Giovanni liked impressing them, no matter how easy it was. The bumpkins.

Most were boys, sun-browned, ragged, unkempt. They wore knee breeches and sleeveless goatskin vests. Some vests still had the long goat hair on them, so from a distance the boys themselves seemed to sprout fur. Don Giovanni took the hair above the boys' ears and twisted it, till it stood in horns. Satyrs. They romped through the herds like kids to make Don Giovanni laugh.

The goatherds' families visited only to seize a goat for slaughter. They hardly talked to the boys. These funny friends of Don Giovanni were valued little more than well-trained dogs. Did they ever forget they were human?

Don Giovanni didn't forget he was. He washed in the river. Most people washed only when their skin grew slick with oil and their hair matted. Every two weeks at most. But Don Giovanni liked the smell and feel of being clean.

He had a second set of clothes now; when one got dirty, he scrubbed it and stored it in a tree hollow while he wore the other. His beard thickened, his hair grew long. But a close look revealed fine features. The peasant girls whose company he was lucky enough to enjoy frequently called him simply by the word *beddu*—beautiful.

His was a world of beauty: orchids, narcissus, jasmine, peonies, in colorful succession and lush profusion. In June he collected wild strawberries that had to be eaten within hours because they spoiled fast—a fault that made them that much more delectable.

In September he left the gathering of the pomegranates to those less able. He eschewed the easy work on the terraced, cultivated lands. He was strong and tough and proud of that. So he went high up Etna's slopes to pick pears with yellow speckles and white flesh, small and crisp with a bite that stung the tongue. Everyone preferred them. He collected pistachios from the trees on the most precipitous cliffs, one by one, dropping them in a cloth sack hung from his neck. A favorite for use in desserts. He was the most fearless worker ever.

But then freak weather came in a burst. Sleet! Sleet in late September! Farmers all of a sudden were saying they had known it would be an early, hard winter. After all, the onion skins were thick; the apple skins, tough. Goatherds knew it, too. Squirrel tails were extra bushy; beehives were extra high in the trees; berries and nuts were more plentiful. Even the town merchants claimed to have known. One man reported having found a breastbone speckled with red in a roast goose. All signs.

Farmers raced to harvest the olives before they got ruined. Don Giovanni wrested the immature fruit from the branches. Everyone said it would be all right: bitter olives made sharp-tasting oil. Different from the usual, but good. They cheered one another on.

Snow came. Then, overnight, there was no more work. The early freeze ruined the orange crop. A whole host of jobs were lost: picking oranges and selling them, drying the peel and selling it. All lost. A man who wasn't a slave or a servant, who didn't belong anywhere in particular, had no way to make a living.

Beggars cluttered the market square. They scattered themselves throughout the town; you could hardly turn a corner without bumping into an outstretched hand.

Once, when Don Giovanni was resting against a wall, clutching his arms against the unseasonable icy wind, a beggar spat on his feet. "My spot. Get out of here."

Don Giovanni was quick to oblige. He was no beggar.

He went back to that first house, that first woman. He offered to collect snow again, from Etna's highest slopes. But snow was plentiful everywhere this year. Just step into the courtyard right after it stopped falling and scoop it up. Besides, she was angry at him, almost as though he'd been an unfaithful lover. Her eyes were bright. Saucy. The way she looked at him . . . why, he'd been a fool not to realize.

It was late October. Don Giovanni had nowhere to go, nothing to eat. The fat times were over, such as they were. He shivered violently.

All Saints and All Souls

"COME HERE, BEGGAR."

Don Giovanni didn't lift his head. He had found a stable door unattended, a rare bit of luck, and slipped in. The dark of a corner allowed him a place to nestle, away from prying eyes, enveloped by this horse's warm, wet, hay-sweet breath. Sleep had already coated him when the rude words scrabbled at the edge of his consciousness.

"You won't regret it, beggar."

The man's voice and language oozed nobility. Don Giovanni was sorely tempted to take the bait. He was hungrier than he'd ever been. He could hear his erratic heartbeat. His skin itched from dryness. The cracks at the corners of his mouth were deceptively small for the pain they gave. He was constipated, irritable, starving.

He needed work. Absolute need. But there was that hateful word; it never failed to jangle his nerves.

"That's a promise . . . beggar."

The lingering of the first words and then the tacking on of the last one felt like a purposeful insult, as though the man knew the effect he'd evoke.

Any true man took taunts seriously. And every Sicilian man was a true man. Don Giovanni looked up.

The man stood by the horse's rump. Even in the meager moonlight from the high window, his fine clothing was apparent. He could pay well. Was the humiliation worth it?

Tomorrow was November 1. Randazzo would celebrate All Saints' and All Souls' Day with morning mass and dancing in the streets. Tonight was the vigil. No one in town had eaten or drunk all day. So tomorrow they would feast. There would be food even for Don Giovanni. He might get a meaty bone if he was lucky. Bread. Maybe even a pastry of ricotta. But it wouldn't last.

And this job would pay well.

"Stop debating and get over here, beggar."

Was he a witch?

Don Giovanni got to his feet. Now he could see the outline of the man's face—unusually handsome. Something stirred in Don Giovanni's middle. A sense of competition? A month ago he had been devastatingly handsome himself. Put a little food in him and he would be again. Handsomer than this dandy.

The man brushed off his cape, ran his fingers through his hair, smoothed his beard to a point. "Good-looking beggar, despite the touch of emaciation. I have to hand it to you."

"You said I wouldn't regret it. Yet already you're breaking that promise. What should I call you, dishonorable sire?"

The man threw back his head and laughed. "Oooo, what style." He made a tsk. "Would you like to be rich again?" He didn't move his hands as he talked. It was as though a statue spoke. "Would you like a life of immeasurable luxury? Beggar."

Don Giovanni willed himself to be a statue as well. The moment felt classic. Recognizable. He could almost walk away from this trap. It had to be a trap. Did Pandora feel like this when she accepted the fateful box?

"Who wouldn't?" he murmured through unmoving lips. Such logical words, each one belying what his heart knew.

"See? Now that wasn't so hard, was it, beggar?"

The man's teeth picked up light that wasn't there. Everything else was in a haze, yet his incisors gleamed. Did he have an internal fire?

He laughed again. "Easy. Let's keep this easy." He reached inside his cloak and took out a purse. A small thing. White as new snow. Rich people would pay Don Giovanni a slab of suckling pig for snow as white as that purse. Or they would have, before nature had stolen his means of survival by dumping snow for free everywhere.

The man lay it on the ground by his feet.

It would surely get filthy now.

"Speak to it." He smiled dreamily. "In the softest whispers, like to your lovers. Say, 'Dear one,' yes, that's the right word, *cara*—dear—such a nice double entendre, don't you think? Say, 'Dear one, give me money.' That's all. Be intimate, caressing. You know how to do it. Name the amount; it will give as much as you ask."

Could this be a hallucination? A vision that comes before death? Had Don Giovanni reached the end so fast?

Starve anyone long enough and visions will come. Great pain does that, too—like from lack of sleep, or torture. Ask any saint. Any of the dozens that would be celebrated in the morning. Or was it All Saints' and All Souls' Day already? Had he been so groggy that he'd missed the midnight church bell announcing the holy day?

He couldn't sense the attention of a host of saints, or even of one saint. But he didn't need them, anyway. Anyone would say the same: This was foreseeable.

"There's a catch, though." The man grinned.

The devil. This vision was a nightmare in disguise. Now came the part where Don Giovanni had to trade his soul.

"No, no, no. You're at once more dramatic and more ignorant than I anticipated. And after all the books you read under Don Alfinu's tutelage." He tsked again. "Not your soul. It would be crude to demand your soul right off. Crude and easy and uninteresting. No, no. Let's do something to banish the ridiculous boredom of ordinary things. Let's start with a test trade. Something much more rare than a soul. Your beauty."

Vanity. The one small indulgence that remained in Don Giovanni's miserable life. Surely the devil could find a more valuable test trade.

"Have you learned nothing? An indulgence held on to so tenaciously—that's the most obvious of opportunities. The profligate way you behaved after you came of age, well, that seemed nothing but the vulgarity of youth. But then you showed me better. The night of the wave. Remember? The way you looked at the maidservant even as her words exposed your hubris. What a source of glee. I still savor that moment. And then the way you looked at old Betta . . ." He laughed. "That was a surprise even for me. But I still had to be sure." He waited.

More bait. Like dead rats for crabs. Don Giovanni should hold his tongue. But in the face of such a fateful decision, explicitness felt necessary. "Sure of what?"

The devil smiled slightly. "Sure that all that desire, all that love, was of yourself, not others. A man who really loves women, all women freely, is the most innocent of all. Foolish, but innocent. Fortunately, that isn't you." He tilted his head. "Who do you think walked into the sea that night? Oooo, the pleasure of seeing you wait for your guests rather than rush into the cold sea to save her. Lust is fun, so long as it doesn't cost you effort. Whose turn of the ankle caught your eye in the middle of a disaster scene? It took you but a moment to leave behind the battered and bleeding to follow your member. Lust is much more fun when it means saving you effort. Exquisite."

Don Giovanni had no saliva to swallow. His Adam's apple rose and fell, dry and painful. He ground the accusations in his teeth—let them become powder, they meant nothing. "Shape-shifter. Stalker."

The devil grinned. "And you wondered at sleet in September. You almost seemed stupid. But your resourcefulness these months has been quite enough to show the contrary. There's no doubt we could have fun. So take the challenge. Prove me wrong. Surrender your beauty.

"Temporarily, that is. Three years, three months, three days. Not so long for worldly wealth, wouldn't you say? In that period you must not wash. You cannot wash yourself, change your clothes, shave your beard, comb your hair. Easy, like I said. Simple. A little wager. A game. And at the end, you even get to keep the purse, with all its magic." He kicked the purse toward Don Giovanni. "But if you break the rules, not only will the charm be broken, but the whole deal is off."

"My soul . . . ?"

"Your soul."

Don Giovanni had experienced poverty for nearly nine months. Like a gestation. From it something akin to desperation was born, shattering the air and any chance of peace with its primal screams. How on earth could it be so damnably hard to climb up out of poverty? He worked and worked, and the next day all that faced him was more work. If he was lucky.

When the weather was good, poverty was, at heart, simply a pointless discomfort. Don Giovanni even enjoyed aspects of it. Waking to the clean spice of perfume from conifers and herbs, the interlacing songs of sparrows, the wavering colors of butterflies and wildflowers. Eating berries as he picked them, fresher than anything had a right to be. Watching eagles float in winds over the mountain.

But when the weather was bad, poverty was hideous.

He should have left Randazzo in late September. He could have gone to the south shore, rocked in the winds from Africa. Or, if he didn't want to wander again, he should have at least prepared for this winter. He could have searched out a cave in the countryside. Lots of people lived in caves year-round. He could have stashed away food for winter. Even dumb animals did that.

Don Giovanni hadn't thought ahead.

Just as he hadn't thought ahead when he'd squandered his fortune in Messina.

What would it be like to be dirty for three years, three months, three days?

He was lucky in a way. He'd gone down to the freezing river just the day before and scrubbed himself from head to foot, even though it made his teeth ache right up through his eardrums. It had taken a good hour of stamping in place to make his blood hot enough to ease the shivers. He'd put on his second set of trousers, his second smock. He'd even washed his cape. He was clean. There was no better way to begin this particular proposal.

And right now, in this very moment, hunger tightened its bones around him. Hard bones. Hard enough to break anyone's spirit.

The philosopher-thief's words came back. This was a wager. A gamble. A game for the hopeful.

And the devil had cleverly posed it in Randazzo, the home of the hopeful. Everyone here had hope. Just living under the shadow of Etna's unpredictable convulsions, they proved that. They looked out on the black, scorched earth after Etna's lava flows and they counted on those little yellow flowers coming again. Maybe not even in their lifetime, but eventually. Hope was a long-term affair.

The flowers' name danced on his tongue: aconite.

On Etna yellow was the color of hope. Yellow butterflies. Yellow orchids.

Was Don Giovanni still capable of hope?

Bong. The church bell. *Bong*.

For the moment existence was only listening to the bells. When they ended, there was nothing. The air died.

Don Giovanni watched his hand move, steadily, as though it were someone else's, controlled by something beyond him. He picked up the purse.

It didn't burst into flames. His hand didn't wither. The purse was flat, empty. A snatch of limp white linen.

Like Saint Agata's veil.

The devil was gone. He didn't leave; he disappeared. A trick of the eye?

"Dear one," whispered Don Giovanni in a tremolo he couldn't control. "Oh, dear one, give me money." How much? How much did things cost? Since he'd left Messina, Don Giovanni had bartered—sweat for food. And before that, his manservant, Lino, and housekeeper, Betta, had taken care of paying for things. "Enough for a room at the inn," he murmured. "Enough for a dinner. An overflowing dish."

The purse swelled. Heavy.

Was he losing his mind? Could this really be?

He pressed the purse to his cheek.

If he left the stable, someone might see him go. They'd secure the doors behind him. And he'd get yelled at. Maybe have things thrown at him. Rocks. Garbage. Yesterday he'd made noise purposely, pretending to try to get into a stable he knew was well locked, just to have that garbage hurled out the window at him. Gnawing at a bone soothed his empty gut.

A dinner at the inn would soothe better.

Who was he kidding? That wasn't the devil. Yes, he spoke as though he understood Don Giovanni's thoughts. Don Giovanni hadn't failed to notice that. But the real devil, not this phony version his demented mind had conjured up, would never bother with someone who looked like him. Like a pathetic beggar.

But then, if the Lord's eye was on every creature, no matter how small, how insignificant, why couldn't the devil's be?

It was possible. Logical. Inevitable.

His fingers fought with the knot on the purse. He opened it. Metal disks. He couldn't see them in the dark, which had become pitch black. But he felt indentations. Arab inscriptions? The Norman royalty in Palermo put Arab inscriptions on their coins.

He closed the purse, tucked it inside his smock, and wrapped his cape tight. He opened the stable door the minimum necessary and edged his way out.

"Thief!"

Thief? No! He clutched the purse through his smock and ran.

Footsteps gained on him from behind. Something grabbed his cape. It ripped.

Don Giovanni sprawled headlong in the alley.

"What were you doing in that stable?"

"Sleeping," said Don Giovanni in his beggar's voice, not moving from the ground. The purse formed a hard lump against his liver.

"It's the middle of the night. If you entered just to sleep, why did you leave now? Eh?" A boot kicked him in the rib. "Turn over."

Don Giovanni turned onto his back. Did the bulge of the purse show? This was his old bad-luck streak coming back in full force. To lose the purse before he'd even used it was a cockroach's luck. A virgin martyr's luck.

The man who stood over him held a long wooden cudgel pointed at Don Giovanni's chest. "I asked you a question."

"I woke."

"What woke you?"

"Hunger."

The man moved the cudgel so it pointed at Don Giovanni's throat. "We're all hungry after a day's fast."

"It's been longer for me," said Don Giovanni.

"Did you take anything from my master's stable?"

"What would I take? There was nothing to eat in there. And I've got nowhere to hide a horse blanket."

"That's true enough." The man rested the cudgel on Don Giovanni's Adam's apple. It hurt. "You're lucky it's All Saints' and All Souls' Day. Mercy rules today. Get out of here. Don't come back. Mercy doesn't rule tomorrow."

Don Giovanni scootched away. The alley was getting him dirty. Dirty already. But as long as he had the purse, he could survive. He got up slowly, hunching over to hide his middle.

"Get out of here!"

Don Giovanni ran.

He went straight to the inn. Closed, naturally. No sane traveler would arrive in the middle of the night.

He filled his hand with pebbles, dirty from volcano soot, and threw them at the front shutters one flight up.

The shutters opened. A lit candle appeared. A face.

Don Giovanni waved to the man. "Hello . . ."

The light went out instantly. The shutters closed.

Don Giovanni scooped up another handful of pebbles. He threw them again.

The shutters opened. "What do you want?"

"A room."

"Have you got money?"

"Yes."

"I'm not coming down in this chill for no reason, am I?"

"It's your business to run the inn," said Don Giovanni. "That's not 'no reason,' right?"

"Where'd you get money?"

"I want a meal, too," said Don Giovanni.

"You've got money for that, do you?"

"Hurry," said Don Giovanni. "Or I'll go elsewhere."

"Sure you will." The man closed the shutters.

Don Giovanni stood in the frigid wind. This wasn't working out. The devil had tricked him. Anyone could have heard his exchange with the innkeeper. Any lowlife out and about in the black of night. At this rate, Don Giovanni would get robbed of the magic purse before he got a chance to spend a single coin. If the purse really held coins, that is. He hugged himself. Where could he go now?

But then the downstairs door opened.

"Show me the money."

Don Giovanni didn't dare open the purse on the road, where anyone could jump him. "Let me come in first."

"No tricks, you hear."

Tricks. On this man's mind. From the devil. Don Giovanni knew about tricks—any starving body did. Just living was a trick. Just not screaming, not falling on the ground and rolling and kicking and thrashing, just holding himself steady like a sane man was a trick.

"No tricks," said Don Giovanni.

The man waved him inside. "Let's see it."

Don Giovanni stood in the hall in the flickering shadows born of the candle's little flame. He took out his purse and dumped it in the man's hand.

The man moved his candle to see better.

They both stared.

Coins. Real coins.

Don Giovanni's tongue went thick with awe.

"This covers a room and a meal, a hearty meal." The innkeeper didn't conceal his surprise. "What did you say your name was?"

"I am Don Giovanni of Messina." The words came in his old speech, that educated speech he'd learned to hide.

"I apologize, sire. I can't heat food at this hour. We have a guest over the kitchen. I mustn't disturb him. You can have cold goat if you want. It's young—*capretto*—or, well, nearly. Eight months old, the little creature—very mild in taste, I assure you. Boned and stuffed with pistachio and rosemary. Basted with wine from Marsala." He held up his candle and peered hopefully through the dark at Don Giovanni's face. "It's a special recipe I learned years ago in Palermo. The king eats it at Easter. There's a loaf of bread—from the day before last, of course; we don't bake during fasting. So it's hardened now. But the oven was fired with lemon branches, always adding that delicate and exquisite aroma. You can sprinkle fresh oil on it. If you don't know our fresh oil, you're in for a treat. Mount Etna's oil is darker and more pungent than Messina's. But this year, with an early winter, it's got an edge unlike anything you've ever tasted. Superb. And you can add salt, fine-ground, naturally. Will that do?"

From some small reserve of irony deep inside Don Giovanni's caved-in chest came the question "No sweets?"

"Figs. Not confections of sugar, no, but these are our sweetest. Roasted black figs with almonds stuck in them. And our almonds—ah, magnificent. The contrast of sweet fig and bitter almond, magnificent."

Don Giovanni didn't trust himself to speak. In his breathlessness, he feared he might faint.

He followed the innkeeper up the stairs.

The Inn

THAT FIRST NIGHT DON GIOVANNI ATE ALONE IN THE DOWN-stairs kitchen. Though he tried to suppress the urge to wolf down the food, he didn't succeed, so the taste was hardly noticeable. In that dim candlelight, it could have been garbage he was eating. It took away the pain in his gut, that's all that mattered.

The next day he ate morning and evening meals in his room, where he stayed sequestered all day. But he went down to the kitchen for the big midday meal.

The inn had two other visitors. There was only one table in the kitchen, a long narrow thing, able to accommodate a dozen easily. So all three sat there, the other two at one end together, Don Giovanni alone. They exchanged initial greetings with him, but that's all.

He listened to their talk. Both were businessmen. One brought samples of silks made in Palermo. He was gathering orders from the seamstresses of the richest ladies in town. He came a few times a year.

The other, also from Palermo, had a bag full of tiny tiles, enameled in brilliant colors. Mosaics. They glistened in the semidarkness of the kitchen, as enticingly as gems. He had come to convince Randazzo that the cathedral needed mosaics on the floor and walls. This was his first visit to the area. At first he told people his tiles rivaled the famous Roman mosaics at Segesta. But many had never visited Segesta, way over in the northwest. So he changed his song. He now said they rivaled the mosaics at Piazza Armerina, not far from the town of Enna. Even though a mudslide had covered that Roman villa a decade before, the nobles of Randazzo had seen them.

Don Giovanni eavesdropped, partly for the comfort of hearing a higher class of talk. His ears themselves were hungry for that. And partly because the information interested him. He had once been firmly ensconced in the world that bought fine silks. He had been among those who would have been dunned for money for cathedral mosaics. Now, with the aid of his linen purse, he could join that world again. If he wanted.

The fact that they didn't address any of their talk to him didn't matter. Don Giovanni hardly cared. He wasn't here for sociability. Eavesdropping was an accidental benefit of the kitchen. And, anyway, he wasn't yet comfortable in his newly regained status. He had to practice assuming the proper haughty tone with the innkeeper or he'd give himself away.

No, he was here in this kitchen simply for food—thanks to the magic purse. His taste buds had come alive again, and the food was good.

The entire following month went much the same. He stayed in his room, except to go to the privy and down to the kitchen for the midday meal. Sometimes he lay in bed and rested. Sometimes he opened the shutters, despite the cold, and sat on a chest pushed to the far side of the room and looked out over the roofs. Sometimes he paced, but always in bare feet. He didn't want anyone to hear him. He'd learned during his months as a beggar that it was rarely good to draw attention to himself. And he didn't want to wear out his skin shoes. They were the ones the woman had given him his first morning in Randazzo, so long ago. They had been in decent condition then. And he'd gone barefoot all summer and much of the autumn, so he had added little wear. Still, skin was skin; their days were numbered.

The rule repeated in his head: *You cannot wash yourself, change your clothes, shave your beard, comb your hair.*

He wasn't entirely sure, but probably new shoes would be counted as changing his clothes. He had to make these ones last three years, three months, three days. Well, less than that now. Days were passing.

No plan had yet come to him of what to do next. But that

was all right. He needed time to gain back flesh and grow strong again. He'd stay in this room, avoid getting dirty, and return to health. Soon enough, he'd think of the next step.

He was slowly getting used to the advantages of money. He made requests for certain foods at the evening meal now. Asked for seconds when he wanted. Addressed a question or two to the other guests, who were growing in number. Yes, he was becoming his old self again.

On a morning in early December, the innkeeper knocked on Don Giovanni's door at the crack of dawn. As usual.

Don Giovanni whispered to his purse before opening the door. As usual.

The innkeeper gave a quick bow of the head to him. "Will you be leaving today, Your Excellency?"

No one had addressed Don Giovanni as "Your Excellency" since the philosopher-thief. The words seemed foreboding, as though there was a joke in the air. A joke at someone's expense. Whose? "Here's payment for another day's food and lodging." Don Giovanni emptied the purse into the innkeeper's hand.

All the preceding days, when the same scene had taken place, the innkeeper had quickly closed a fist around the coins. But now he looked at them and hesitated. "Will you be staying in again all day?"

"Yes."

The innkeeper tucked the coins away somewhere inside his shirt. He went to the window and pushed the shutters open.

The bright sun of a cold morning slashed in, dividing the room into the lit and the dark.

The very act felt like an invasion to Don Giovanni. This was his room—he'd paid for it. He controlled every aspect of it. He stiffened. "Close the shutters, please."

The innkeeper took the cloth looped through his belt and brushed ash off the windowsill. "Christmas is coming soon," he said as if addressing the world outside.

"I said close them. Please."

The innkeeper turned and gave Don Giovanni a mirthless smile. "I thought the light might cheer you up."

"I don't need cheering. I'm taking a chill."

"Perhaps you need warmer clothing. I could fetch a tailor."

"No. No, thank you." Don Giovanni walked to the window and reached past the innkeeper. He pulled the shutters closed.

The room seemed darker than before. Shrouded.

The innkeeper lit the oil lamp. "He's a reliable man, this tailor. Discreet. He'll take care of your needs."

"I don't want new clothes. And I don't need discretion."

"Something more appropriate. Clothes that suit your station in life."

"These are my clothes," said Don Giovanni, smoothing both hands down the front of his smock. "These are what I wear."

The innkeeper smirked. "Well, if you insist, why don't you

strip down? I'll have my maidservant mend and wash your clothes."

"No, thank you."

"It would do you a world of good. Then you could go outside."

"It's not my clothes that stop me from going outside," said Don Giovanni. "I don't want to go outside."

"We can bring you a basin and fill it with nice warm water for a bath." He spoke quickly, his lips moving like swarming insects. "Sheep tallow and large salt grains do a world of good in refreshing the body and soul. And a scrub brush made of boar hair."

"No. I said no. No, thank you."

The innkeeper pressed his hands together in front of his chest, fingertips pointing up, the backs of the fingers of one hand touching the backs of the fingers of the other hand. He shook them.

Don Giovanni recognized the gesture as one of exasperation. "What's it to you what I wear, whether I'm clean, how I pass my day? I pay for my lodging. I pay for my food."

"People come through town at this time of year. The inn fills up. It's full already. People are sharing beds."

Don Giovanni crossed his arms at his chest. He knew what was coming now, it was all too clear. But if he stood like a statue, maybe he could bully this innkeeper. "And?" He lifted his chin so he could look down his nose at the man.

"They like the place to feel festive. To match the spirit of the season. They dress well. They're businessmen of a certain class."

"So am I."

"Yes, Your Excellency. And what is your business?"

"I don't have to explain myself to you. It's rude of you even to ask."

"Rude? This is my inn. Your behavior here is my concern." The man shook his hands in that gesture of exasperation. "Your Excellency, you are a fine gentleman. I know that. But you don't dress like my other visitors expect. I get complaints."

Don Giovanni bristled. "Clothing doesn't make the man."

"That's true." The innkeeper's chest swelled with slow, deep breaths. He looked at Don Giovanni appraisingly. "Perhaps it wouldn't be that hard to appease them if we did a little grooming. A shave. A comb run through your hair."

"Appease?" Don Giovanni stepped backward, as if slapped. All he'd done was direct a couple of questions at a visitor or two. And the pretentious blockheads had complained? "I don't make trouble for anyone."

"You sit at the kitchen table. They don't want to sit near you."

"The table is long," said Don Giovanni, but he knew he'd already lost this argument.

"With more people coming over the next couple of weeks, they won't be able to avoid you. And no one will share a bed with you, of that I'm certain."

Don Giovanni turned his back to the innkeeper. He whispered inside his smock to the linen purse. Then he reached in and took its contents and turned around. "Here." He threw coins onto the bed. "Double the usual. I'll pay double every day from now on."

The innkeeper's eyes flickered to the money and back, but he didn't jump at it. "This is not such a fancy inn, to merit that kind of pay. Maybe you'd prefer to continue your travels and stay at a better inn, in some larger city. Most of the best places are far in the west, in Palermo, of course. But if you wanted someplace closer, you could always return to Messina. That's where you said you came from, right? Am I right?"

"Yes," said Don Giovanni grumpily.

"I hear it's been rebuilt after a wave and it's more hospitable than ever."

"This inn suits me. This is where I want to be."

"Your Excellency, I'm not worthy of this honor."

The words raised hackles on the nape of Don Giovanni's neck. A spark of panic shot up in the backs of his eyeballs. "I have to stay."

"People talk," said the innkeeper. "If word gets around . . ."

"What word? That there's a man in ordinary clothes with a beard?" Don Giovanni forced a laugh. "That's some big scandal, all right."

"A recluse in questionable clothing." The innkeeper shook his head and looked at the floor. "I'll lose business. There are two other inns in town."

"What? You want more money? Is that it?"

The innkeeper's head jerked up. "Where do you keep all this money?"

"That's not your affair."

The innkeeper looked away, then back at Don Giovanni. "Triple pay for as long as you stay."

"Fine."

"And you take all your meals in this room."

"Fine."

The innkeeper gathered the coins from the bed and held out his hand for more.

"I'll give the rest to you later," said Don Giovanni.

"How much later?"

"After the morning meal."

The innkeeper left.

Don Giovanni blew out the lamp and took off all his clothes. He stood in the dim light and felt his arms and legs and chest and belly. He was almost back to his summer self in size. Yet right now he had the sensation of being reduced to something insignificant, vulnerable. Like a small animal who had wandered by mistake into a large cave.

This was just the beginning of the game. It shouldn't be hard yet. Don Giovanni had no excuse for feeling so depressed. He chanted the rules under his breath: *You cannot wash yourself, change your clothes, shave your beard, comb your hair*. These rules had to be his religion for the duration of the game. He must win.

Don Giovanni felt his hair. It formed knots here and there, but it wasn't the matted mess that many beggars' hair was. If the visitors at this inn had really complained about his grooming, they were way too persnickety. His clothes, yes, they were regrettable. But his person, no. He was relatively clean.

Still, Don Giovanni himself didn't like those knots. He worked his fingers through them. Did fingers count as a comb? He let his hand drop. He'd get used to knots. They were nothing in the larger scheme of things.

As for his clothes, well, generally, though they were peasant clothes, they were reasonably clean and in good shape. He had managed to brush off most of the dirt from when he fell in the alley the night he got his magic purse. Maybe he should let the maidservant mend the tear in his cape at least. After all, "change your clothes" meant "put on a new outfit." It didn't mean "alter your clothes." He couldn't be breaking the rules if he simply had the cape sewn. Could he?

But the devil enjoyed double meanings. He'd stood in the stable and called the purse "dear," and remarked on his own cleverness. Words were part of his game.

There was no point in risking it. A rip in his cape was tolerable.

So the upshot was that there was nothing to be done. No

changes. Triple pay would satisfy the innkeeper. And Don Giovanni was happy enough to take all meals in his room. The food was good; that was the issue to focus on. He couldn't let anything else matter.

In fact, now that he wouldn't be going down to the kitchen for the evening meal, he wouldn't have to wear his clothes when he ate. He didn't have to risk getting food on them. So he was better off. Ha!

Indeed, he could stay in his room naked all day and all night. He'd slip on his trousers only to answer the door when the maidservant brought his meals and to make a dash for the privy.

He could live like that for the whole game period if he wanted.

Witless though he was, that cowardly innkeeper had provided Don Giovanni with a plan. Don Giovanni could pay him to bring books. He'd pass the day reading. And watching the world from his window. If he got restless, he could run in place.

Don Giovanni shook out his cape and draped it neatly over the writing table. From nowhere came the calculation of days; it was December 8. His birthday! The new plan was a birthday gift.

He stretched out his smock and hung it from the stool, pulling tight to get rid of all the wrinkles. He laid his trousers across the chest at the foot of the bed and pressed them in perfect lines. He put his shoes under the window, where they could air out.

Then he whispered to his purse. He poured the coins onto

the bed and marveled at them. Maybe he'd never get used to this. Magic disoriented him.

There was a knock at the door.

Don Giovanni pulled on his trousers and opened the door to find the innkeeper himself holding the tray of food, rather than the maidservant who usually brought his morning meal. Well, of course. The man was eager for the money.

The innkeeper looked at the table, covered by Don Giovanni's cape. "Where should I put this?"

Don Giovanni took the tray. "Your money's on the bed."

"I see it." The innkeeper took the money. He looked around the room quickly and with a touch of—what, suspicion?—he left.

Don Giovanni set the tray on the floor. He took off his trousers and folded them onto the bed. Then he sat by the tray, naked. He broke the stale bread into pieces and dropped them into the bowl of hot goat milk. He cut up the raw onion and dropped it in, as well. This was the same breakfast he'd had his first morning in Randazzo, with the exception of the added onion. And it's what he'd eaten any chance he got during his months of begging.

He could have had soft, fresh cheese with sugar stirred into it, and just-baked bread. Or a chunk of hard bread with a slice of roast meat from the day before. That's what the other inn visitors had in the morning. It's what Don Giovanni used to eat, back in Messina. But after his first two mornings of that here, he'd asked for this peasant breakfast instead. It's what he'd eaten with the goatherds all summer and autumn. He'd come to prefer it.

Surely that marked him as different, as well. A recluse in questionable clothing. That's what the innkeeper had called him. A shady character. With lower-class culinary habits to boot. Well, he'd show that innkeeper. Don Giovanni would order a fine cake for this evening. His personal birthday celebration.

The goat milk had the same effect on him it always had. He finished the last drop, pulled on his trousers, and ran for the privy.

On the way back, he met the innkeeper coming out of his room.

"What were you doing in there?"

"Straightening things, Your Excellency."

"The maidservant straightens things."

The innkeeper pursed his lips. "This is my inn. It's my responsibility to check the rooms."

He was a good enough liar in voice and words, but Don Giovanni saw the shiftiness in his eyes. The innkeeper had done something secret in Don Giovanni's room. Sneaky.

His purse!

Don Giovanni quickly pushed past the innkeeper into the room. The purse lay on the bed. The smock and cape were where he'd left them. But everything was slightly different. Telltale details. A fold in the cape, but he'd smoothed it flat with both hands. The smock a bit to the right, but he'd spread it precisely over the center of the stool. And the purse open, but he'd drawn the strings.

"Everything's in order, as you can see," said the innkeeper behind him.

"Yes."

"And, oh, would you mind paying for the next two weeks now?"

"Paying ahead? Why?"

"That way I won't need to disturb you so often, seeing how much you value your privacy."

"I'll pay by the day," said Don Giovanni, "like all your other guests."

The innkeeper put out his hand. "I think it would be best." His eyes gave him away again. Despite his courteous voice, this was a challenge.

He'd searched the room. He'd found no money.

And Don Giovanni stood before him in simple trousers with no pockets. No place to have stashed money on his person.

Curiosity must be driving the man to distraction.

"All right," said Don Giovanni. "But I'll pay after the midday meal."

The innkeeper nodded and left.

Don Giovanni paced. Then he dressed and went out into the street.

Lord, it was cold. He pulled his cape tight.

The innkeeper had talked of two other inns in town. Where? In all his months here, he'd never had occasion to search for an inn. He had known of this one only because it was so close to the stable he liked to sneak into.

He turned to retrace his steps and faced a girl, not fifty paces away, whose mouth formed a dismayed O. He knew her; she was the maidservant who brought his meals to his room. She spun on her heel and walked away quickly.

Don Giovanni ran to catch up.

The maidservant looked over her shoulder in fright. She ran, as well.

A short, wide fellow stepped out of nowhere into Don Giovanni's path. "Are you bothering that young woman?"

"Get out of my way," said Don Giovanni. He had to catch the girl.

"I'm not moving for no beggar." The man put his fists on his hips. Then he squinted up into Don Giovanni's face. "I know you. You mucked out my master's stables last spring. You look different without that red ring around your eyes—you'd been a snow gatherer before you mucked out manure, right? Eyes tearing all day from Etna's fumes. The worst jobs in the world, they were yours. So who do you think you are, talking stuck-up like that, telling me what to do? You mess with that young woman and I'll beat you senseless."

Don Giovanni drew back in alarm. He was stronger than

this man, no doubt about it. But he wouldn't do anything that would get his clothes dirty.

Besides, he didn't want to chase the girl anymore. What was the point in catching her and telling her not to follow him? The innkeeper would just send someone else to do it. That man was determined to find out where Don Giovanni got his money from.

It was time to leave Randazzo.

The Donkey

IT WAS MORNING. HIS BELLY WAS FULL. AND THOUGH THE AIR was cold, the sky was clear. If Don Giovanni had to leave the city, these were as good a set of conditions as any.

So long as he had the magic purse, he'd be all right. And a birthday was an auspicious day to make a journey. Twenty years old. He could take on the world.

He stood on the road outside the town walls. To the east, the only cities of enough size to have inns were Catania and Messina. But Catania was under constant threat from Etna, and Don Giovanni had had it with the Mountain.

Messina was an even worse choice. No matter how careful Don Giovanni was, his clothes and body were bound to get dirty and dirtier. He didn't want anyone who knew him from before to see that. Especially since he planned to return there when the game was up and buy back his castle and refurbish it more extravagantly than ever.

He set out westward in long strides. There was no point in being sluggish about it. Besides, vigorous motion would raise his body temperature.

Within a few kilometers he was surprised to find that the land on both sides of the road was relatively free of snow. The explanation came almost immediately, in a fierce wind that swept dead leaves and twigs and dirt in his face. He put up his hood, wrapped his cape tighter, and forged ahead, bent into the wind. But the chill made him need to urinate. Though there was no one in sight, these roads were curvy, and travelers could appear out of the blue. So he couldn't relieve himself in the open.

Well, he'd be quick about it. He dashed off the road toward a stand of trees and within a few steps he sank deep. He knew immediately what it was—not a snow pocket but a gully of soft ashes. It was impossibly stupid of him not to have been on the alert for it. The texture of ashes was recognizable to anyone who'd lived here even a month. And the wind had brushed the snow so thin on this slope that ash gray showed through, dull stains in the middle of the shiny white of snow dust and the black glitter of frozen dirt. Ash absorbed the sunlight like cloth soaking up water. Anyone should have seen it. What a dunce he was.

He walked back to solid ground. Soot covered his shoes and clung to his trousers up to mid-calf. Stupid stupid stupid him.

He returned to the road and stamped his feet, lifting his

knees high, trying to shake off as much as he could. Then he urinated right there in the middle of the road.

A man leading a donkey came up a side path at that very moment. He didn't bother to look away. Rather, he stared. Maybe he'd seen Don Giovanni jumping around. Maybe he'd even seen him sink into the ashes. Now an idiotic grin filled his face.

Embarrassment made Don Giovanni mean. "Are you as dumb as you look?"

The man laughed. "Are you?" His laugh was actually good-natured.

He passed. On the donkey's back was a pile of stools tied together by a thick rope. It seemed a haphazard mess, some upside down, some sideways, though Don Giovanni knew the arrangement was a careful balance. Why, there might have been ten or more stools there. The comical burden was higher than his head. That little donkey was strong.

"Wait," called Don Giovanni.

The man didn't slow down.

Don Giovanni hurried back to him. "How much do you want for that donkey?"

The man grinned again. "What are you, a comedian?"

"How much? I've got money."

The man gave a hoot. "Not enough."

At the sound of the man's laughter, the donkey turned his head. But the pile of stools stuck out on both sides and blocked his view. So he turned around, looked the two men in the face, and swiveled his oversize ears toward his master. He was a smart animal, Don Giovanni could tell.

The man continued along the road, leading the donkey behind him again.

Don Giovanni let them get far enough away that he was sure they wouldn't hear. He turned his back and whispered into his smock, "Dear one, give me money. Give me the wildest sum this man could possibly want for his donkey." The purse filled to an amount that was pathetically small. How poor was this man, anyway?

Don Giovanni closed the coins in one hand. He ran after the man. "Name your sum."

"I've got to deliver these stools to Randazzo this morning. Don't slow me down."

"Think of the wildest sum you could possibly want for your donkey. Hold out your hand."

The man smirked, but he held out his hand.

Don Giovanni filled it.

The man stopped. He counted the coins. He counted again. Then he frowned and gave the money back to Don Giovanni.

"Isn't it enough?"

"I can't deliver the furniture without my donkey."

"Then deliver it. I'll wait here and take the donkey when you get back. And you can bring me something to eat for mid-day, too."

"I have only enough food for myself."

"I'll give you money to buy food. Enough for you and me both."

"More money, eh? You've got more money than that?"

"Not much," said Don Giovanni. The man didn't look shrewd enough to try to rob him, but appearances could deceive. "Just enough for the donkey and a meal."

"I need my donkey," said the man.

"You can get two for that price," said Don Giovanni. He watched the man's face and knew; he added, "You could get three."

"This is a good donkey," said the man. "He never gets sick. He never balks. The next one could be different. Then where would I be?"

Was everyone in this part of the world greedy? The innkeeper wanted triple pay. And now this donkey owner wanted to fleece Don Giovanni, too. It didn't matter that he had an infinite source of money. It was the principle of the thing. It galled him to be cheated.

On the other hand, who knew how long it would take him to get to another town of decent size going west? He didn't want to dirty himself any more than he already had. And maybe the man was right; this donkey did seem special. Don Giovanni would have this donkey, whatever it took.

"How much do you want?"

"How much have you got?"

"This is absurd," said Don Giovanni. He put the coins back in the man's hand. "Return with the donkey and food, and I'll pay you a fair price."

"A fair price beyond this?"

"Yes."

"And I get to name it?"

"Within reason, yes."

The man put the money in a bag around the donkey's neck and left.

Don Giovanni stood watching them go. They were remarkably slow. Still, he knew donkeys could keep up a trot for long periods. If he rode, he'd not only stay clean, he could travel much faster than walking.

He looked around for a spot to wait. A large rock sat off to the side. He picked his way carefully through the dry rubble of dead weeds only to find that the rock was covered with a layer of ash.

He really was sick of Etna. Fire and snow: no worse combination was imaginable.

He wouldn't try to venture around the ash pit again. And the next closest stand of trees was a fair distance from the road, uphill all the way. But he had time.

He climbed to a pine, broke off a low bough, and went back to the rock. He brushed it clean, every nook and cranny. Then he sat down.

The winds grew sharper, coming from two directions now.

Maybe a storm was on the way. He put up his hood again and nestled down inside the cape, cursing its thinness.

How long had the donkey man been gone? The sooner Don Giovanni got that animal, the sooner he could start his journey. Trot, trot. A donkey trot was fast. He just had to remember that; he had to keep telling himself. A donkey trot was fast.

But not fast enough.

All right. When he passed someone on horseback, he'd trade in the donkey for a horse. That would be easy enough. With a horse, he could go all the way to Palermo in a matter of days.

In fact, it was ridiculous to sit here waiting for the donkey man. He should go back to Randazzo and buy a horse immediately. Who cared about the money he'd already given the donkey man? He had to start thinking differently. The purse made everything different.

Don Giovanni walked toward Randazzo fast.

Two men came along the road. They were talking loudly to each other. They hushed when they saw Don Giovanni. They drew closer to each other.

Don Giovanni nodded greeting.

"That's the one, isn't he?" said one man to the other.

"I'm pretty sure."

The men blocked Don Giovanni's path.

"Give us your money," said one. He was missing so many teeth, the words came out with a whistle.

Don Giovanni's heart sank. There was no way he could produce a coin without giving away the secret of the purse. "I don't have any."

"Sure you do," said the whistle man. "The money for the donkey."

Don Giovanni kept a blank face. "What donkey?"

"We heard him describing you," said the whistle man. "In the tavern, eating a meal he says you paid for. Singing and drinking. He bought everyone a round. You're the one, all right."

"I don't have money."

The other man pulled a knife from under his cloak. He held it high in his left hand, like a torch.

Don Giovanni took off his cape. He shook it out in front of their faces. He folded it and set it on the ground. The new wind whipped through his smock, as though it were made of spider gauze. He clenched his teeth and pulled the smock over his head and shook it out so they could see. He folded it and set it on top of the cape. His chest was goosebumps. He took the purse from its spot inside his waistband and opened the drawstrings. He shook it, turned it inside out, then laid it on the pile of clothes. "Nothing. You can see."

"Take off those trousers."

Don Giovanni didn't bother to argue. He took off his trousers, shook them, then laid them beside the pile. After all, he didn't want their soot to dirty the rest of his clothes.

"And your shoes."

He took off the shoes and shook them out.

He stood there naked, pressing his knees together, hunched against the open cold of the Mountain, which was ten times fiercer than the city cold. "I told you."

The other man whispered to the whistle man.

The whistle man made a humph of agreement. "Where'd you hide it?"

"I didn't have anything to hide. I swear."

The other man whispered to the whistle man again.

"You were sitting on that rock over there," said the whistle man. "Did you hide it there?"

"I didn't hide anything. I swear on the memory of my mother."

The other man punched Don Giovanni in the stomach.

The air went out of him. It was a stunning blow. He doubled over. For a moment he couldn't see anything. Then his eyes found the knife again. Still in the puncher's left hand. Ready.

"Where is it?" came the whistle in his ear.

"I don't have anything. I swear on the Blessed Virgin."

Another blinding punch to the gut. He fell to his knees. A crippling chop on the back of his neck. He was on all fours. His stomach wrenched. Vomit came out his mouth and nose at the same time. A kick in the thigh. He lay flat now, snuffling in the pool of vomit.

"That'll teach you to make false promises. We came all the way out here for nothing." So much whistling in his ear. "Your mother's a whore. But you're lucky we respect the Blessed Virgin."

Don Giovanni managed to turn his head so his nose and mouth were open to the air again. A high-pitched hum, like the whine of mosquitoes, prickled on his ear and cheek. It spread across his lips and chin, up his temple, across his forehead. It grew loud now, a din. There was nothing to do but listen to it.

After a long while, the hum faded, and senses returned in the crudest way. His nose told him he had defecated. His hands and feet told him he was dangerously cold. His spine seemed frozen. It was as though a sword of ice had been jammed from his anus to his throat.

He pushed himself up, leaning on his hands. Once he was sure he was steady, he reached one hand behind to feel his shoulder where he'd received the blow. The hand came away dry. So it hadn't been the knife, thank the powers that be.

He looked up the road. How was it that no one had come along in all this time? Randazzo had constant business, yet no traveler had passed to help him. A decent traveler, a God-fearing soul, would have picked up his unconscious body, washed it, treated his injuries. And not a bit of that would have broken the wager rules, for Don Giovanni would not have been responsible.

Don Giovanni turned in a circle. No matter which way he

turned, savage wind was in his face. Wind to keep charitable travelers home. Wind from four directions at once. Unheard of. Like sleet in September.

"Cheater!" he called out.

"Were you addressing me, beggar?" A tall man, impeccably dressed, appeared on horseback. His horse pawed the ground spiritedly, but he held the reins steady and looked down at Don Giovanni with a slight tilt of the head. His face was actually regal. And so normal-looking, so human. Don Giovanni wouldn't have recognized him for sure—after all, he'd only seen him once before and that was in the dark of the night stable—except for his eyes. Those dead eyes.

"Only the weak cheat!" Don Giovanni walked as close to the horse as he dared. "Is that what you are? A weakling?"

The man's jaw twitched.

"Your winds kept home the wicked, too, not just good folk. No other scoundrel came to do me more harm. Your vicious winds saved my life. So the joke's on you."

The man smiled and there were those glowing teeth again. "Should you die before you break the rules, you're lost to me."

"You broke the rules, cheater!"

The man leaned past his horse's neck. "Your pathetic little rules don't bind me."

Don Giovanni shook his fist. "I can take this. Even if you cheat. I'm made of firmer stuff than you think."

The devil sat back upright and wrinkled his nose. "It's only too obvious from your odor what you're made of. Onward, beggar." And horse and rider were gone. Vanished.

Don Giovanni was alive. It didn't matter that the devil wanted him alive, too. He was a mess—but an alive mess, and that was a good thing.

His clothes lay where he'd left them. Another thing right.

And the purse was there.

He needed to put those clothes on fast. The cold undid him. But he wouldn't let himself dress, filthy like this. He'd soil his clothes. *You cannot wash yourself, change your clothes, shave your beard, comb your hair*. How could he get clean without washing?

A technicality. That's what he needed.

Washing called for water. Without water, it couldn't be washing.

He wiped one hand in the dirt of the road, getting it as clean as possible. Then, with his two cleanest fingers, he carried his clothes, piece by piece, to the rock. There at least they would be out of harm's way.

He climbed back up the hill to the pine tree. He crumpled pine needles into scratchy wads and rubbed himself all over. He wanted to rub till he was raw and red. Instead, his skin turned slowly blue.

The stink of vomit and feces hung over him like a curse, but he had to give up. Whatever still clung to him would have to be endured. He was too cold.

He went to the rock and dressed. His teeth chattered so hard, he thought they'd break. Then he'd go around whistling, like the bully. His laugh ended in tears.

The sun was growing weak already. The winds never ceased. He let them push him, as he made his way slowly back toward Randazzo.

Cani

HE WOKE WITH A START AND SHOOK HIS HEAD.

"Yip." The dog jumped backward.

Don Giovanni sat up. It hurt to move. He was battered and bruised. The cold had stiffened his joints. The smell of his own face made him gag. He looked around.

The dog stood with his front legs splayed and his chest lowered, his eyes fastened on the slow movements of the man. He was ready to dash away at the first threat.

Don Giovanni put a hand to his cheek, where something had disturbed him. It was wet. He understood instantly. He leaned forward. "Come on, Cani—Dog—come on. You can trust me. We've slept here together more than once. You remember the old days." If only Don Giovanni hadn't pushed the dog away in those days. He sweetened his voice. "Come on. Do it again." He practically sang, "Please."

The dog came forward slowly. He gave a tentative lick. Then another. Need stilled every muscle in Don Giovanni's body. Enormous need. This is what prayer was.

Don Giovanni closed his eyes and pressed his lips together. The wet rasp went over his eyelids, up his nostrils, in his ears. A tongue can be a miracle of strength and yet flexible, one of the Lord's great inventions.

The old proverb went through his head: *Tutti li gusti sun gusti, rissi lu iattu liccannusi lu culu*—"All tastes are tastes, said the cat, licking his anus." He'd laughed at that disdainfully when he was a boy. Never again. With each movement of that dog's tongue, gratitude swelled the man's heart a little more. *Keep it up, Cani. Please.*

Now there was tugging at his beard. The dog was trying to get a piece of vomit free from a snarl of hair. It hurt. But he wanted the dog to be successful. And, anyway, this pain was nothing compared to the ache in his stomach and back from the punches the day before. He braced himself so he wouldn't tumble over at the quick, wrenching moves.

But then, "*Aiii!*" Don Giovanni opened his eyes and jumped to his feet. He touched his chin. His hand came away bloody.

The dog had run to the other side of the alley. It looked at him with worried eyes. A clump of Don Giovanni's beard hair stuck in his teeth. It made him look rabid, but also slightly comical.

"It's all right. Come on back. Come on, Cani." Don Giovanni held out a hand and bent forward.

Cani slowly crossed the alley.

Don Giovanni patted him on the head. "You didn't mean to do it. I know that." He went down on one knee with a small groan and gingerly touched the hair hanging from the dog's mouth. When the dog didn't growl, he yanked it free and threw it away. "I owe you, Cani. I smell like stinky dog breath now. That's better than vomit."

Cani licked Don Giovanni's hand. Slowly. Meticulously. Now his wrist. He worked his way up the forearm, the elbow. Cani's head was under his cape now, licking higher.

Don Giovanni pulled away, shocked by his own initial passivity. If he didn't set limits, the dog would lick him in his private places. Then he'd be no better than an animal.

Every single thing was a potential trap, for what good would winning the wager be if he lost his humanity?

It was almost morning. He spoke to his purse. He shook a coin from it and leaned against the wall to wait.

The milk boy came up the alley, leading his four nannies.

"Here." Don Giovanni held out a coin.

The boy blinked. A wary look crossed his face, but he didn't back up. "What for?"

"Milk. For me and him." Don Giovanni motioned with his thumb at the dog, who had retreated to the far side of the alley again when the goats came into sight.

"Milk doesn't cost that much," said the boy.

An honest boy. Someone who wasn't greedy. Don Giovanni wanted to kiss his feet. "If you give us our fill of milk every morning, I'll give you a coin once a week."

The boy looked around. "Where's your jug?"

"Squirt it into our mouths."

The boy took the coin and it disappeared somewhere inside his cape. He put down the bell he carried. "Who should I do first?"

"Cani." Don Giovanni called, "Here, Cani, come on." He slapped his thigh. "Come on."

Cani hurried over.

The boy took a goat teat and squirted Cani in the face.

Cani shook his head in surprise, but that dog caught on fast. He opened his mouth and licked at the stream of milk as it came through the air.

Don Giovanni got on his knees. The boy squirted him now.

Good milk coated his innards as it went down, taking away the pain. "Enough." Don Giovanni closed his eyes and stayed like that. Within seconds Cani was licking the milk that had squirted onto Don Giovanni's face and beard. And licking the bloody wound, too.

"I'll bring you a bowl tomorrow."

Don Giovanni opened his eyes wide at the unexpected words of kindness. "Thank you."

But the boy had already gone ahead to the house door. He clanged his iron wedge.

Don Giovanni limped quickly to the corner and turned down the next alley before the door opened. He looked behind. Cani was at his heels.

This was a good start. Something he could build on.

They got into a routine, Don Giovanni and Cani. The milk boy filled their bowl twice in the morning—one bowlful each—for a coin a week. The maidservant who swept out the kitchen at a house on the next street over gave them a loaf of bread every dawn for a coin a week. They split it, half and half.

Their midday meal was in a tavern in the German Lombard section of town. The owner was a vintner of considerable reputation and the more prosperous people went there to drink, gamble, sing, visit prostitutes. Don Giovanni had never entered the establishment during his beggar period, so no one knew him. Anonymity felt safer.

He couldn't understand most of what the German tavernkeeper said, but it didn't matter. He put his coin on the table and the tavernkeeper put in its place a plate of hot food. Usually stew of mutton or goat, but sometimes chicken or boar or venison. And always lots of greens.

The whole thing was spiced with cinnamon or ginger or pepper. Lightly. Delicately, in fact. The cook knew his trade. And the wine was a pleasure, made from the huge grapes that grew on Etna. People said they were the largest in the world.

Don Giovanni responded appropriately with his most polite habits. He cut the meat off the bone into small pieces and delivered them to his mouth either on the point of his knife or in the spoon. He never rushed. He took his time chewing, savoring the cook's mastery, sipping the wine, letting it roll slowly across his tongue.

Cani stayed under the table busy with the gristle and knuckle and bones. But when there was venison, well, that was different. Cani loved venison. Don Giovanni would buy a second plate and put it on the floor for the dog, even though he knew that producing two coins was risky. A single coin, well, a beggar might luck upon that by catching the eye of a particularly generous person or finding some small job. Even on a daily basis. But two, that raised suspicions.

Don Giovanni indulged himself in that risk partly because it gave him satisfaction to see Cani so overjoyed. The dog gave evidence of a miserable life before he'd joined up with the man, clear evidence: he'd come to expect nothing. Every time Don Giovanni slipped him a bit of nerve or sinew under the table, the dog was as excited and grateful as the first time it had happened.

And Don Giovanni indulged in that risk partly because he needed one tiny declaration of bravery—only now and then—just to let himself remember, even if poorly, how bold he once was, how bold he planned on being again. He tapped the purse inside his smock. *Three years, three months, three days.*

For the evening meal, man and dog satisfied themselves with a bowl of bean soup and dark bread to dip. They ate this outside the kitchen doors of one of a dozen different homes where the cook had agreed to the arrangement. One coin fed them both for two nights running.

And, again, the man was on his best behavior. He ate with the same habits he'd use at a banquet table. It was important to maintain the semblance of being civilized whenever possible. Because he was civilized. Don Giovanni was a human being, with a soul.

He recovered from his beating quickly. After all, he'd gotten into good health during his stay in the inn, so he had a solid foundation to build on. He felt lively again.

The more amazing thing was the transformation of Cani. His eyes turned alertly to every sound, every motion. The frightened, frantic dog that had run back and forth beside Don Giovanni that first night he'd come to Randazzo, way back last February, was completely gone. This new version of the dog seemed curious, intelligent, interested in the world. But never interested enough to stray. Oh, no, he stayed at Don Giovanni's heels, even when cats crossed their path. He was a disciplined dog. Don Giovanni admired that in him.

At first Don Giovanni tried to get the two of them on a nocturnal schedule. During the day they slept between meals out in the open in the largest market square. No one would dare attack them with all the traffic going on. At night, they wandered the streets, staying close to the buildings, noticed only by the rats. They keep their eyes peeled, constantly on the lookout for thieves and hoodlums.

But Cani was spooked by the shadows of night. His eyes weren't good in the dark. He barked his worries and people shouted at them and threw things from windows.

Finally, Don Giovanni had to admit that Cani wasn't ever going to adjust. The dog was willing, Heaven knew that. He'd try anything Don Giovanni suggested. But dogs aren't nocturnal. So they had to go back to walking all day, and sleeping under the staircase at night.

It turned out all right, though, because Cani put on flesh quickly. His black coat glistened. He was sleek and robust, and his appearance alone commanded respect, just as Don Giovanni had hoped. No one bothered them as they slept. Only a fool would risk angering that dog.

And Cani wasn't a bad blanket, not bad at all. They made it through Christmas and January and February. The coldest time of the year. It was working.

"Another pact," said Don Giovanni when he'd scratch the dog behind his ears. "A holy one, this time. We take care of each other."

But all good things come to an end, as Don Giovanni looked at it these days. So on the mid-March afternoon when the German tavernkeeper pushed Don Giovanni's coin back at him and gestured for him to get out, he wasn't surprised.

Over the past month, there'd been a gradual transition. At first Don Giovanni ate alone at one end of a table, with Cani underneath and other eaters at the far end. Then people got up and moved to other tables when he sat down, even if it meant crowding. Then the table nearest to his would empty, too.

Without being asked, he'd taken to sitting in the corner spot, to displace the fewest customers possible. It was only a matter of time until the tavernkeeper barred him.

He looked a fright, after all. He could see it in the eyes of children, in the way their mothers pulled them closer and sped up as they passed him. And he stank. He reeked. He was a putrid sack of filth. There was no other way to put it. He hated his own stench. He'd taken to breathing through his mouth, to diminish the nausea he caused himself.

It was one more irony. As Cani had grown more handsome, Don Giovanni's appearance had deteriorated. The dog kept himself clean everywhere with his tongue, but the man allowed that tongue to explore only his face.

The odor from his bottom was the first to become overwhelming, thanks to that beating from the bullies. Then the odor from under his arms ripened and turned rancid. And then his feet developed the most peculiar condition. They grew scaly on the soles, and raw between the toes. They itched constantly and radiated a foul odor.

His back itched, too. And his chest, where little, red, angry-looking pustules had formed. And his ears. He wondered if maybe insects from Cani had migrated into them. In fact, he itched all over. Even his scalp. Especially his scalp.

So he couldn't blame the tavernkeeper. Don Giovanni was

bad for business. And he'd learned from experience that it only made things worse if he offered to pay extra.

He waited outside until the midday meal was over. Then he went in again.

"Out," said the tavernkeeper, pointing with his whole arm at the door Don Giovanni had just walked through.

"I could eat around back, by the kitchen door," said Don Giovanni. "No one would see me. I'd pay the same."

"What's the matter with you?" The tavernkeeper spoke Sicilian as he shook his head in disgust. It surprised Don Giovanni, who hadn't realized the man knew the language. "Clean yourself up, man."

"I can't."

"You're a disgrace. I don't want your money the way you are now. Clean yourself. Act like a God-fearing man again, and you can come back. But not till then. Don't hang around here. Go."

Man and dog walked through the streets. They went to the staircase that sheltered them at night. In the corner under it, behind a small pile of rubble, was the bowl the milk boy had given Don Giovanni. He filled it with coins. Maybe when the boy came looking for them in the morning, he'd find it.

Then they stopped by the doors of all the kitchens that had sold them morning bread or evening soup. It wasn't obvious what would make a good hiding place—one the maidservant or cook was likely to look in but that others wouldn't—so Don Giovanni simply left handfuls of coins hidden under rocks or rubbish, whatever he figured the maidservant or cook might be asked to sweep away.

As a final good-bye, he handed a coin to every beggar they passed. Just one. There was no point in inviting trouble.

They went down the main street of town and out the gates to the road again.

"It's all right," Don Giovanni said to Cani. "The meat meals in that tavern were over anyway. It would have been fish stew all through Lent till Easter. And you're not much of a fish eater." He scratched behind Cani's ears. Then he scratched behind his own. Then he laughed. What was the point in not laughing? It was spring. "It was time for a change anyway, my friend."

The Heart of Sicily

IN SPRING THE INTERIOR OF SICILY FROM ETNA TO PALERMO rivaled the Garden of Eden. Sweet sage perfumed the world. Heavenly.

So long as people were avoided, that is.

People had their charms, it was true. They had so many different customs, just from one village to the next. Don Giovanni liked watching them from a distance. The women, of course. He would never stop admiring the beauties of women, how they fluttered so decorously. The devil was wrong—his love of women wasn't narcissistic. Indeed, he had no delusions about being attractive anymore. So his persistent appreciation of women despite the absence of any chance of carnality disproved the devil's claim.

Three years, three months, three days. The first thing he'd do when the time was up was scrub himself new. The second and third and fourth and . . .

But he also liked watching the men. Here were hats that sat like an overturned bowl on the head, there were ones that hung down at the rear like the sack of an octopus body, and over there were ones that poofed out high above the head like a church bell. Each little isolated mountain town was a world unto itself. Don Giovanni had no sense of what the differing habits of clothing meant. He would have liked to ask someone, but on the increasingly rare occasions on which he'd speak, people shied away from him, if they didn't outright run.

People meant other good things, as well. Music. All Don Giovanni's life he'd enjoyed street musicians as much as the refined musicians who performed chamber music at the banquets in his castle. Randazzo had offered him plenty of the former. The towns in central Sicily that he wandered through after leaving Randazzo offered him more of the same. A simple little tune plucked on a Jew's harp could bring a wide smile to his lips. In the towns with Muslim residents, the cane flutes held notes that wavered in the air like calls to prayer. He loved the bagpipes and the triangle and the drums and the tambourine. He would step back into the shadows and watch dancing for as long as it went on. Or as long as no one chased him away.

People meant cooked meals, prepared sometimes exquisitely, letting off aromas that made his mouth water. Sheep cheese flavored with saffron to a deep yellow—ah, he had that in the mountain town of Enna outside the door of a Muslim home. He made Cani wait across the road before he knocked. He had learned that Muslims hated dogs. They used them for hunting and guarding, but never as pets. And they especially despised black ones like Cani. But he saved the last bite of the cheese for the dog. That was their rule—share.

He had egg drop soup in Enna, too. Scrumptious. Even a simple round loaf of bread came to seem inordinately delicious.

People meant gardens whose walls Don Giovanni peeked over to admire beds of roses, and delicately fragrant sweet peas. Musky trefoils, ranunculi, fan palms, and Judas trees with their flaming canopies, all arranged to please the eye. Once he watched a troop of slaves pass an entire day trimming graceful curves in hedges.

People meant an occasional innkeeper, typically needy for business, who let him spend the night in the stable, if not in a room.

People meant gaily painted carts. Children playing stick games in the alley. Pottery that seemed to caress whatever it held. Fountains carved with nymphs and sea horses. Butchers and farmers who called out their goods. Oh yes, those merchants' calls.

And that was it: Most of all, people meant language. This island of Sicily was rich in tongues. Some of what Don Giovanni heard, he couldn't understand. Some he understood, but only in the vaguest way. Understanding it himself hardly mattered anymore, though. Hearing people talk to each other, seeing them respond with joy or sorrow, that was the marvel he witnessed, nearly awestruck every time.

That was the most painful loss: without language it was hard to remember he was human.

But contact with people had to be avoided, for people also meant senseless brutality. Not just toward others they looked down on: slaves and beggars—the misfortunate who were blamed for their own misfortune—but also animals, creatures who couldn't possibly bear blame.

Don Giovanni watched a horse-drawn cart near Enna one day in mid-spring. The old mare had undoubtedly served as her master's reliable mount until the years caught up to her and landed her here, in this very different type of work. A white lather of sweat swathed her neck and withers. One leg bled profusely from high up, near the rump. Her muzzle was red, her nostrils dilated, her eyes despairing. The man leading her slapped her hard with a cane to speed her up. She would die in her tracks one day. Simply drop there. For her sake, Don Giovanni hoped it would be soon.

People kicked dogs and threw hot oil at cats. People beat donkeys and prodded goats with pokers.

In his old life, that fantasy life in the castle, Don Giovanni had rarely given a thought to animals beyond considering their usefulness to him. Now how someone treated an animal was the first thing he noticed. He wouldn't take a chance that someone might hurt Cani.

The dog impressed Don Giovanni with his intelligence, goodwill, and loyalty. Probably no one had recognized that in him before Don Giovanni came along, or Cani never would have been left to fend for himself.

Don Giovanni figured his newfound appreciation of animals also came from the fact that an outsider sees things an insider is blind to. Or, rather, he notices what he sees; he gives attention to different details. Observing those details lent a quiet dignity to the role of outcast. Don Giovanni spent his days watching the world. Counting the days until the wager was over made the pain seem longer. But gathering details, reveling in them—that filled his brain so that sometimes he truly lost track of time.

The wild horses that lived in the Nebrodi Mountains, for example. They were worth study. Many times Don Giovanni wasn't certain which direction to go in the wilderness. Some directions led to impassable precipices. Some became slopes that were too steep or had rocks so loose they slid out from underfoot. Some went nowhere near water. He quickly learned to look for hoofprints. Horses invariably made paths through the most easily passable terrain. And horses always led to water eventually. Downright clever.

Plus, horses were a thrill to watch. Their deep brown hides glowed reddish in the sun. They'd run hard and work up a lather and their hair would slick close over rippling muscles. They were everything a healthy body should be, everything Don Giovanni used to be.

So he and Cani mostly avoided people and stuck with the animals. They lived in the wild through the rest of that spring and the first part of summer. The times when the valleys were lush. Instead of the flutterings of women, they had butterflies in orange and black by day, and moths in blue and white by night. For music they had the evening chorus of cicadas, but also sparrows, robins, nightingales, magpies. The birds were so lyrical, sometimes Don Giovanni was sure they were singing just for him and Cani. For gardens they had wood asphodels and astragalus and so many other wildflowers, and the white, gaudy blossoms of caper bushes. For food they ate berries and greens and chewed on fennel. They trapped rabbit and beaver. They caught eels and crabs. Cani made sure they steered clear of porcupines and boars and snakes and wildcats and weasels and martens.

It was as close to Eden as a man without a woman could find.

But by July most streams had dried up. It wasn't like on Etna, where streams flowed year-round. The heat of central Sicily was unrelenting. Dirt rose as the finest dust—not a hint of water in it. The sun threatened to split the rocks. Don Giovanni and Cani were forced to stop their random wanderings and seek water from reliable sources.

Lakes were the obvious choice. They were few and far between and small, but Don Giovanni was delighted to find that he and Cani learned their locations easily. It was like a homing instinct. Whenever Don Giovanni's tongue would get fat with heat, whenever he was sure that this time he'd pass out before they managed to slake their thirst, they'd stumble out onto a perfectly cool patch of blue water in the middle of woods, with wagtails and coots and mallards and kingfishers cavorting. What a fine thing to have this gift.

Oh, Don Giovanni was no idiot. It wasn't luck that made him find lakes. It wasn't some beastlike instinct. He was led to them. The devil was protecting his wager. But that knowledge never made the discovery of a lake less welcome. Joy was joy, and Don Giovanni was learning that a little humility didn't ruin it.

He knelt beside Cani and the two of them lapped water companionably. They looked at each other and a message of relief passed. It was strange, but Don Giovanni knew it was unquestionably true: he and Cani were best friends. Friendship so deep and true was new to Don Giovanni. When they sat under the stars, with Cani snapping at fireflies, he felt nearly peaceful.

It must have been August, a full year and a half since the wave, when Don Giovanni found himself staring into clear water at a man who didn't look the least bit peaceful. A wild man. Head hair stuck out in long clumpy locks, so thick and snarled it was impossible to disentangle one from the others. Facial hair covered cheeks, protruded over lips, hid any hint of a jawline. It came down past his neck, past the hollow at the base of his throat. All that showed through that furry mess were half-crazed eyes, a grimy nose, and the inner rim of a cracked lower lip.

He held his arms out slightly away from his body because the boils in his armpits hurt if he lowered them. He'd worn through his shoes a couple of months ago now and he favored his right foot because of a cut that oozed pus. Each night he'd press out the guck, but by morning it would be swollen again. It simply wouldn't heal.

And the itching. He'd dig his fingers through his matted hair and try to get at the source of it. He'd roll on the ground and scrape his back and chest to try to rid himself of it. Day and night. Itching.

And there was all that water. Cool, cleansing water.

He stared. The wild man stared back.

Who had the crazier eyes?

You cannot wash yourself, change your clothes, shave your beard, comb your hair.

Was swimming washing himself?

No, swimming was swimming. It wasn't washing.

Except if he went swimming in order to get rid of some of this filth, then it was washing. And that's exactly how he had cleaned himself during his nine months of poverty before the devil came to him. He'd bathed in the rivers. So swimming was washing.

Or was it?

Don Giovanni turned his back and took a few steps away through the crackling grasses. The ghastly heat made the air waver. It carried his stinking sweat like a cloud. All he could smell was his own decay.

If he didn't think about washing, if he just kept his mind focused on swimming, then that's all he'd be doing. Swimming.

He turned back around and waded into the water up to his calves.

Cani didn't need further encouragement. He splashed past Don Giovanni gleefully and paddled out to the center of the lake, disrupting the peace of the mallard family. They took to the air in noisy quacks and came down again at the far tip of the lake.

Don Giovanni stopped. He felt beyond time, as though floating in some place that didn't exist. He looked around, taking in the details in this windless moment. Secrets hid in the details.

Klu-kluklu-kluee. An eagle rose from a tree on the other side of the lake. Don Giovanni had seen pairs of these brown birds before, but they'd been silent. Something had disturbed the bird. Something was still disturbing that bird. He soared in a wide circle, crying. Birds of prey were harbingers of bad news. But the eagle was the symbol of Palermo, of the strength of Sicily. A double message. How to make sense out of it?

Cani turned abruptly in the water and let out a growl.

Instantly Don Giovanni jumped out of the water.

Swimming would have cleaned him. He knew that. He knew it, he knew it, he knew it. No matter whether he managed to control his brain so that he thought only of swimming, he knew. That's what counted.

He trembled. How close he'd come to the precipice.

"Trickster!" he screamed.

The devil appeared beside him, as pristine and handsome as ever. "Do you really believe it's necessary to scream? I hear your thoughts . . . beggar."

The eagle was still crying. And Cani's growls grew louder as the dog swam fast toward his owner.

"Do all animals hate you?"

"One eagle and your groveling dog, and you jump to the conclusion that all animals hate me." The devil lifted his chin. "You really have become provincial quickly, haven't you?"

"You didn't deny it. So they do. Every animal knows you're filth."

"Filth? Oh, nothing could be sweeter than hearing you, of all people, call someone else filth." The devil hissed in his ear, "Stupid beggar, people are animals and people don't all hate me. You have no idea how many are drawn to me. But you will." And he disappeared just as Cani came out of the water.

Don Giovanni sat on the shore, one leg bent, cradling his sore foot, and cried. Never had he been more grateful. The wager was still to be won. It had to be won. He couldn't go through all this only to lose.

He sat rocking himself for hours while the dog sniffed through the undergrowth then, finally satisfied that no danger lurked, romped happily again.

When night finally brought a bit of respite from the heat,

they set out at the fastest pace they could manage. Lakes were too dangerous. Town wells were the only choice.

They had traveled across the heart of Sicily many times by then, but they had eventually gravitated toward the northwest. They were in the well-wooded Madonie Mountains, the next-highest peaks to Mount Etna's. Don Giovanni's goal was Palermo.

Palermo was the answer. The city had well over twenty thousand people, almost double Messina's population. They ranged from dirt poor to the king, from raving lunatics naked in the alleys to the most refined scholars and statesmen in their carriages. Don Giovanni had seen them himself. He had visited the city twice as a young baron. Everything and anything was possible in such a place. If there was anywhere on earth Don Giovanni could pass in his present condition without drawing too much attention, it was Palermo.

Originally he had planned to hold out in the woods until the cold of winter forced him to the city. But now, with the lack of fresh water, they had to make it to Palermo quickly.

They came out of the wilderness onto a road and followed it downhill. Moonlight reflected soft off white pebbles. There was a sense of suspension about the night, as though a breeze was just about to start.

A wagon came along, pulled slowly by a donkey. A man and woman sat on the front bench. The woman was wrapped in a head scarf and long sleeves. Only the tips of her shoes showed. Muslims.

Muslims could be counted on for charity.

Don Giovanni ordered Cani to stay in the bushes while he went to stand in the center of the road. He stretched his hands out, a coin in each palm.

The man pulled the donkey to a halt.

"Please, sire," said Don Giovanni. He came up closer so the man could see the money. "A coin for food. A coin for water."

The woman didn't look at him, but she reached behind and talked to someone. Don Giovanni made out the figure of a curly-headed child back there. A bundle in a small swatch of cloth passed hands, child to woman, woman to man.

The man held out the package. "Drop the coins in my hand, but don't touch me."

Don Giovanni dropped both coins in the man's hand.

The man dropped the package in Don Giovanni's hand.

"Water?" asked Don Giovanni.

The man shook his head. "We have nothing to give it in. One jug. You can't put your lips there."

"I'll buy the jug."

"With what?"

"Wait." Don Giovanni went toward the side of the road and turned his back. He put the cloth package on the ground and whispered inside his smock to his dear purse.

Cani came slinking from the bushes, tail wagging, clearly unable to bear waiting any longer.

Ruff! Rrrruff rrruff rrruff.

But it wasn't Cani barking.

The wagon hurried past them up the hill and now Don Giovanni could see a large spotted dog tied to the rear. He barked like an idiot, jumping around, trying to get free, as though he wanted to tear the throat out of the night shadows.

He practically flipped over himself when he saw Cani. His barks became totally enraged.

Cani raced after the dog, meeting the challenge with his own.

"Come back, Cani," called Don Giovanni. He ran after the dog.

The wagon driver shouted at the donkey to go faster. The woman turned around and clasped her arms around the child and stared with a terrified face at Cani and Don Giovanni, as though they were the devil incarnate.

"Cani, Cani," called Don Giovanni. If only the cut in his foot didn't hurt so bad, he'd be able to catch up. "Please, Cani."

Cani stopped and looked at Don Giovanni. He gave a last ferocious bark at the dog and wagon, and returned to his friend.

The wagon creaked away. Don Giovanni watched the night swallow it and absentmindedly scratched behind Cani's ear. Water was in that wagon. Lost now.

For a moment quiet prevailed. Then the cicadas took up their song again, hesitant at first.

Grrrr! Cani raced toward the bushes.

Don Giovanni's skin formed goosebumps. This was the growl Cani used with wildcats and weasels. "Leave it be, Cani," he called.

But the dog was already bounding into the bushes.

"*Aiii!*" A man came running out of the bushes, straight toward the flabbergasted Don Giovanni. "Here." He shoved the cloth package into Don Giovanni's hands and hid behind him.

Cani came running at them.

"Call him off, call your dog off. For mercy's sake!"

Don Giovanni stood between the man and Cani, arms outstretched. He felt giddy. No one had asked him for help in so long. This man was a thief; he'd picked up the bundle of food that Don Giovanni had paid for. He'd undoubtedly meant to make off with it. But it didn't matter; Don Giovanni was happy. He bent down and hugged Cani in his confused joy.

The man backed away. He turned and walked fast.

"Come back," called Don Giovanni.

The man walked faster.

"Come back or I'll set the dog on you."

The man stopped and turned around.

"Let's see what's in this package." Don Giovanni held it out.

Cani sat at his feet, eyes on the package.

The man watched.

"Feels like there might be enough for three here." He sat in the road. "Come sit with us."

The man walked back slowly.

Don Giovanni started to unfold the cloth, then he thought better of it. "Do you want to open it? Have a seat."

The man sat. His knees stuck out to the sides like broken wings. His arms were sticks. He opened the cloth carefully.

They shared flat bread and balls of salted cod mixed with finely chopped onion and celery and parsley and pepper and—what were those sweet bits?—raisins and quinces.

"Arab food is good," said Don Giovanni.

"Mmmm. I get it almost every night."

"You steal it?"

The man wiped his mouth with the back of his hand. "If I have to. Usually I just beg."

"And you get meals like this?"

"Not in this quantity, no. But tasting like this. The only travelers on this road in the middle of the night are Arabs."

"And why's that?"

"Palermo's been unfriendly to them for a while now. Most have moved outside the city. But they come at night, just to the outer walls, to meet with those Christian merchants who will trade with them. Which is almost all, of course. Business is business." The man fell silent.

Don Giovanni wanted him to keep talking. It was so fine to

be talked to. "I never saw a Muslim wagon with a dog tied to it before."

"They all have dogs now. For safety." The man stood. "Thanks for the meal."

"Wait." Don Giovanni got to his feet. "What about water? How do you get water?"

"At the public fountains. But you have to bring your own amphora." He walked off the road.

"Wait. What's your name?"

"If we meet again, I'll tell you." And he was gone.

Cold desolation enveloped Don Giovanni. Talking with that man, that combination of beggar and thief, had been exquisite. Like fine wine after a bite of aged cheese. A prize.

He used to talk with the goatherds that summer he spent on the slopes of Mount Etna. They'd tease and tell stories and laugh. But somehow he'd never even tried to talk with beggars. And they were such an obvious pool of potential contacts. None he had seen was as totally shabby as Don Giovanni. But they weren't clean, either. And this one hadn't said a word about his odor. He hadn't looked askance.

Maybe there was more to look forward to in Palermo than just water.

One Year Done

HIS STOMACH CRAMPED. FOR THE PAST MONTH DIARRHEA HAD ravaged Don Giovanni. And he knew the cause. He'd seen it in his stools. Worms. Somehow worms had infested his body and settled into his gut. Cani had them, too. Which one had given them to the other, Don Giovanni didn't know. Or maybe they'd both gotten them from the same place.

His foot had healed, though. And, really, trading that pain for worms was a good deal. Worms didn't hurt. They were an annoyance more than a danger. If he hadn't had enough to eat, it would have been different. But these days he had plenty to eat. Anytime he wanted. He'd go have a meal right now, in fact.

He got three metal coins from his purse and tucked it back away. Then he stretched and came out of the stable.

Zizu ran up. "Don Giovanni, you're awake." The boy danced around him.

Cani joined in the play.

"Ready to eat?" asked the boy.

Don Giovanni gave Zizu the coins. "Something hardy."

The boy ran off.

Don Giovanni went down the narrow alley and relieved himself in the open sewer. The gutter had been used by lots of people already today. Don Giovanni knew it stank, but his nose had ceased to function. It was a godsend in some ways; it allowed him a little distance from his predicament. But it had its drawbacks, too. For one, he could hardly taste food anymore. He ate in order to stay strong, that's all.

Zizu was waiting by the stable when he got back. The boy carried a little satchel tied to one wrist and a jug in both hands. He put the jug on the ground and opened the satchel, which contained three cheese-filled pastries with pistachio nuts on top.

"Arab food?" asked Don Giovanni.

"Only the Jews and Arabs are selling today. Christians are fasting."

Of course. It was October 31, the vigil of All Saints' and All Souls' Day. Don Giovanni smiled and the corners of his dry mouth split, but the little burst of pain didn't stop his happiness. Tonight would make one year since he'd entered into the wager. Only two years, three months, and three days to go.

Two years, three months, and three days.

Don Giovanni stopped smiling. Two more years of this torture.

"Aren't you hungry? If you don't want this, I can go into the woods and gather mushrooms. The yellow kind you love. And wild asparagus."

Don Giovanni looked down. Zizu stood holding a pastry, his eyes intense. Cani's front legs were slightly splayed, and his eyes bore through Don Giovanni, too. The other two pastries lay in the open satchel on the ground. Zizu and Cani were waiting for Don Giovanni to take his pastry before they ate theirs. He was the master.

The grand don. The master of a dog and a beggar boy. Well, actually, three beggar boys. There were Kareem and Giancarlu, too. They were a little older and they showed up erratically.

The boys never touched him, they never smiled at him. Sometimes they smiled when he gave them more money than expected, but that wasn't at him, that was smiling to themselves.

Cani, now, Cani stood near him and licked his hands and slept beside him. Cani would have smiled at him if dogs smiled. He wagged his tail at him. He was always delighted to be with him.

At this moment Cani was still watching him intently.

"Sure, I'm hungry. We can get mushrooms another day." Don Giovanni picked up his pastry and took a bite. After all, he was a benevolent master.

Zizu and Cani ate greedily.

Don Giovanni ate slowly.

Two years, three months, three days.

Zizu went into the stable and returned holding the three bowls that were stacked in Don Giovanni's corner, along with his blanket. He filled them each with coffee from the jug.

Zizu and Don Giovanni drank theirs while Cani lapped his. The dog showed no hesitation at coffee. It made him practically spring off the ground for the better part of the day, but if he didn't like it, he didn't show it. He was a funny dog that way; Don Giovanni was convinced Cani would try anything if he sensed Don Giovanni wanted him to.

Implicit and total trust. And loyalty.

Don Giovanni could do it. He would make it through the next two years, three months, three days. He had to. And when it was over, he'd make sure Cani had everything he wanted for the rest of his life.

Don Giovanni walked through the streets slowly. The cold ground worried him. Winter hadn't yet snarled down the alleys this year, but it would. Soon. Getting new shoes counted as changing clothes; the wager precluded that. And without shoes, winter might wind up making a prisoner of him in that stable. No light. His main source of pleasure, watching the world around him, would be gone.

Alternatives seemed lacking. Every inn he'd approached in Palermo had turned him away. Well, who cared? The boys would bring him and Cani meals, so long as they relied on him for their own meals. And with his blanket and plenty of straw, a stable offered almost as much as an inn, given that if he'd succeeded in getting into one, he'd certainly be confined to his room.

Who was he kidding? An inn room had a window. It was far superior to the stable.

All right, then. Everyone said the coastal road west offered fine views of the rocky shore. He mustn't be stupid and waste whatever time remained before frigid rains came. He'd feast his eyes, then feed on the memories during the winter months of visual deprivation ahead.

Cani raced up and down through the alleys, always coming back to check on Don Giovanni's progress on the main road until they reached the westernmost of the four city gates. Palermo had grown so much in recent years that the city had spilled beyond the walls, so that there were many homes even here. But soon enough the dog was chasing birds and rabbits up and down the hillside, again coming back periodically to the coastal road to make sure the man was still there.

It was during one of those stretches when Cani was off chasing something or other that Don Giovanni saw the cove. A short, narrow sandy beach curved in a cupid's bow, with vines growing down the rocky walls. Boulders just offshore made it inhospitable to larger boats. And its size made it undesirable to groups. A perfect lovers' cove.

On the other side of the road, set back some distance, was a large villa. It was a surprise to see a noble's home isolated like this. To the side of the front door a stone bench waited in the sun. Don Giovanni answered its call. He went up the path and sat on it.

He was right. The bench was situated perfectly to take in the view; someone had undoubtedly built this villa right there because of that cove. Perhaps the owner was a painter?

Don Giovanni pulled his feet up onto the bench, crossed his ankles, and let his knees fall out to each side. He reached a hand up under his trousers from the bottom and picked bugs from the hairs on his calf. He crushed them against his thumbnail and flicked them away. A mindless task. Sometimes he'd pass hours this way.

A gasp came from behind him.

Don Giovanni turned his head to see a woman lean from a window. A servant, by her clothes. She gave him a look of dismay and disappeared inside.

A moment later a man peered down at him from the window. The master, clearly. He disappeared inside, too.

Don Giovanni watched the door. One of them would come out soon. They'd offer him money to leave.

It was useful, this reaction. Don Giovanni had heard the beggar boy Giancarlu explain to Zizu and Kareem one time that this was the source of Don Giovanni's never-ending supply of coins. That assumption kept his purse safe.

Don Giovanni held out his hand to accept the inevitable coin.

But he was wrong. The master stood at the window again. From the look on his face, he was afraid to get too close. Well, that was no surprise. Most people seemed to be afraid of Don Giovanni these days.

"Go away!" The man pointed down the road back toward the city. He spoke a haughty French. "Nasty beggar. Leave!"

"You're the one being nasty." An impishness tickled its way across Don Giovanni's chest. He wrested a clot of something or other from his beard, smiled at the disgust-filled face of the man, and tossed the bit of crud toward the window.

The man jumped backward into the room, then reappeared, his face pinched with anger. "Filthy beggar!"

"You're not only nasty, you're wrong. I'm not a beggar, though the mistake is understandable, given that I had my palm out." Don Giovanni was using his natural diction, that of a Messina baron. True Sicilian. It let this Norman know he was the real intruder here, on the noble island of Sicily. Watching the shock on his face made Don Giovanni grin. He smoothed his mustache away from his teeth, so the man could see his enjoyment. "If I wanted, I could persuade you and your wife to leave this lovely villa." Who knew if the man even had a wife, but Don Giovanni liked the sound of saying that.

"Absurd." The man laughed. His courage had obviously

come back from wherever it had been hiding. "Exactly how could you do that?"

"Money. Sell me your house. I'll buy it this instant."

The man shook his head.

"Name the price."

The man opened his mouth as if to speak, then he seemed to think better of it. He stepped back from the window. When he returned, he said, "All right. Let's go see Don Cardiddu."

Don Giovanni breathed shallowly. Had the villa owner truly taken his offer seriously? What changed his mind? But it didn't matter. All that mattered was buying this place. How absurd that he'd never thought of buying some place before. He wiped his beard away from his lips. "And who is Don Cardiddu?"

"Only the most respected lawyer in all Palermo. I entrust him with all my dealings. We can have a contract drawn up. Follow me. But not too closely."

Could this be real? The man's tone was at once condescending and self-congratulatory. Still, Don Giovanni didn't see how it could be a trick. A lawyer was a lawyer. A contract bound those who signed it, no matter what their station in life.

The man went on horseback, slowly.

Don Giovanni followed on foot. Cani had rejoined him, and the dog stayed close now. Frequently he looked up at his master with curious, alert eyes. Each time, Don Giovanni gave him a pat on the head.

The lawyer Don Cardiddu was a burly, jovial type, who hesitated only a moment at the sight of Don Giovanni, then dutifully produced a contract. When the gentleman, Don Muntifiuri, named his sum, the lawyer blinked in astonishment. His face said it all: The villa wasn't worth that much. Perhaps no villa was.

To the ordinary buyer.

Don Giovanni quickly signed. According to the agreement, the money must be paid eight days from the signing. Then the villa would be his. A home again. Complete with furnishings, stable, horses, servants.

Don Muntifiuri reached for the plume. His hand was white, a stark contrast to Don Giovanni's, whose nails were so dirty it seemed like he'd dipped his fingers in pitch. The gentleman's shirt was white; face, white. His hair glowed white now. The sun seemed to come from behind him, bleaching him to a cloud, a wisp, a memory of a man. While Don Giovanni was a shadow of a man. Neither of them real.

Don Giovanni rested both his hands on the lawyer's desk and leaned there for support. He felt energy flow out of him like water through a sieve. He was going to faint. When he came to again, all of this would be gone. The dream, vanished. White and black, annulled. He hated himself for having a dream that would haunt him so badly in the months to come.

But Don Muntifiuri signed.

And Don Giovanni didn't faint.

"Eight days." Don Muntifiuri folded each hand under the

other armpit. "You come up with all those sacks of gold and the villa is yours."

"Mind that it happens just so," Don Giovanni managed to say, appealing to the lawyer, who looked back at him with what seemed an honest face. And he went outside to lean against a wall and catch his bearings.

This was his chance.

What he needed now was a room. A large one. Only an inn could serve. But he couldn't go to any that had already shunned him.

He headed for the Jewish section of town. His stomach had announced lunchtime already anyway, and it was sure to be business as usual in the Jewish quarter. Jews observed fasting and feasting days, but different ones from the Catholics. They couldn't care less about the vigil of All Saints' and All Souls' Day.

Don Giovanni and Cani wandered through the entire quarter before they selected the biggest and undoubtedly most expensive inn. Don Giovanni whispered to his purse, "Dear one, give me money. Enough to pay for every guest bed in this inn for a week, three times over." He clutched the gold coin that fell from the purse into his hand. It had the head of an emperor with a crown of laurel leaves. He used to have so many coins just like this; it must have been minted in Messina. He called out to the innkeeper.

The man came outside. "What do you want?" He held himself straight, his hands clutched together in front of his chest.

Don Giovanni stepped back the distance he had learned it took to make people less anxious about him. "How many empty rooms do you have?"

"That's no business of yours."

"It could be . . . if I took all of them."

The man turned to go inside.

"For a full week."

The man stood with one hand on the door handle. "You don't have the money."

"I assure you I do. How much would you want?"

"Who taught you to speak like a gentleman?"

"My mother," said Don Giovanni. "My father. Who taught you?"

The man shook his head. "Even if you had the money, I couldn't let you in. My other guests would protest."

"How many guests do you have?"

The man swallowed and his Adam's apple rose and fell. "Only one. But more are coming next week."

"I'd stay one week only and leave on the eighth morning. Your guests wouldn't even know I'd been here."

The man wrinkled his nose. "They might."

Don Giovanni was stung, even after all this time. "You could scrub the room down with vinegar after I left." He shrugged companionably. "That's easy enough, right? I'll pay for the entire inn. For one full week."

"Every bed? You'd pay for every bed?"

"That's what I said."

"Why?"

"Isn't it easier for everyone that way?"

"It's a danger to my reputation," said the innkeeper.

"How much would it take to make that danger worth it?"

The innkeeper didn't speak. Maybe he was calculating sums in his head.

"Think of the price you want." Don Giovanni came a step closer.

The innkeeper stepped back.

Don Giovanni put the gold coin on the ground in front of the innkeeper's feet. "Exactly right, wouldn't you say?"

The inkeeper stared at the coin. He picked it up. "But . . ."

"I'll take my meals in my room."

The innkeeper nodded.

"In fact, I'll use only two rooms. One next door to the other. So if you want to rent out the remaining rooms, you're free to do so."

That night Don Giovanni laid his purse right inside the door of the empty room next to his own. He carefully stretched out the drawstrings so they extended past the threshold of the door. "Dear one," he whispered, "give me money. Fill this room with gold coins."

For the next seven days, Don Giovanni wouldn't leave the inn. He couldn't take the risk of someone coming upon his purse in action. He knew his three beggar boys would be looking for him. They'd miss the meals his coins paid for. Especially Zizu. He imagined the small boy's stomach twisted in hunger. Indeed, when he'd first come upon the boy, in September, he was nothing more than skin and bones. He probably wouldn't have made it through the winter if Don Giovanni's coins hadn't put a little flesh on him. But there was nothing to be done about it now. The purse had to be guarded. Everything depended on a white linen purse.

On the eighth morning, Don Giovanni reached two fingers under the door of the room next to his. He could feel coins. And under them, at the end of the drawstrings, was a bit of cloth. Linen. He pulled it out and tucked the purse inside his smock. Then he ordered Cani to sit outside the door and wait for him.

He went downstairs.

The innkeeper rushed to meet him. "It's the eighth morning."

"Don't fear. I'm leaving." Don Giovanni went to the door. "But not immediately. I'll be back within the hour with a couple of gentlemen. In the meantime, please bring Cani his breakfast. He's waiting outside the door to the room next to mine."

Don Giovanni went to the lawyer's home. To his great relief, Don Muntifiuri was there already.

Don Muntifiuri laughed. "You showed up. Empty-handed. I knew you didn't have the money."

"But I do," said Don Giovanni. "You'll need several carts. Don't worry, you can call for them later. For now, come with me to count it. And you, lawyer, please accompany us."

"Nonsense," said Don Muntifiuri. But he followed anyway.

They went to the inn. The innkeeper preceded them up the stairs. When Don Giovanni opened the door to the room next to his, gold coins spilled out into the hall. The room was full, floor to ceiling.

"Take what you want," said Don Giovanni. "It's more than we bargained on."

"It was a joke." Don Muntifiuri looked at the gold dumbly. "I never meant to sell my home."

"Buy another," said Don Giovanni. He willed his voice not to crack. Everyone had to stick by their bargains; he mustn't show any doubt. "We have a contract."

Don Muntifiuri picked up a handful of coins. He stared at it in disbelief.

"Bite it." Don Giovanni turned to the lawyer. "See for yourself; it's real. We have a contract."

"He's right," said the lawyer. He pocketed a coin without biting it. "Don't act like a fool, Don Muntifiuri. You can buy any home you want with the money here. Why, the entire room is crammed with gold sovereigns."

Don Giovanni took the house key from Don Muntifiuri.

"Come back anytime," said the innkeeper as Don Giovanni walked past him with Cani, out into the street, toward the coastal road.

Christmas

MORE THAN A MONTH LATER, ON CHRISTMAS MORNING, DON Giovanni stretched out on the ground in the center of the courtyard of his villa, surrounded by the porticoed colonnade, and closed his eyes.

Cani flopped down beside him. The dog had been out running since dawn, so he panted noisily. His breath came in warm bursts over Don Giovanni's nose. It offered respite from the damp chill of the air.

Zizu and Giancarlu and Kareem had gone off to Holy Mass in their new clothes. Kareem wasn't even Catholic, but he enjoyed the spectacle, he said. And they all wanted to show off their new station in life. Exactly what that station amounted to was hard to say. They slept in a room of the villa. On their own beds. They came and went whenever they wanted. They had food and clothing. These three boys had tended to Don Giovanni's needs for his two months on the streets of Palermo, when no one else would help him. As far as he was concerned, they could live here as long as they liked.

The mistress of the maidservants who had worked for Don Muntifiuri quit immediately after the sale of the villa. All the maidservants under her left, as well. No other maiden, young or old, could be found to take their places. But a young man had finally agreed to be cook. Ribi. He was a quiet sort, who entered rooms only after Don Giovanni had left them. If Don Giovanni needed something from him, Zizu carried the message. Ribi was competent in a number of ways. Not only was his food delicious, he'd managed to rid Don Giovanni of worms with a week's regimen of garlic and hot peppers. And he never mentioned it. Don Giovanni appreciated that discretion.

Right now Ribi was in the kitchen preparing the holiday feast for Don Giovanni, the three beggar boys, and Cani. Once it was on the table, he was free to go home, to pass the rest of the day with his family, about whom Don Giovanni knew nothing.

The menservants from Don Muntifiuri's days had stayed on, since Don Giovanni doubled their salaries. They kept the stables and falconry in order; Don Muntifiuri had been quite a hunter. They watched over the terraces of olive trees and repaired the supporting rubble walls, for the property had a large and prosperous olive oil mill. They would tend the small field in spring. And they maintained the villa and answered the door.

In the first weeks, answering the door was a task. Guests came to welcome the new baron to the area. Some of them were genuinely friendly. Some nosy. Some were opportunists. It turned out that both Don Muntifiuri and the lawyer, Don Cardiddu, had engaged in gossip: everyone had heard of the inn room overflowing with gold sovereigns.

The rush of activity surprised Don Giovanni. The announcement of each new visitor made his cheeks hot with hope. The potential for friendship, no matter how unlikely, was at its maximum, given all these new people.

And when an invitation came for a feast in Palermo on December 8, Don Giovanni felt dizzy. Someone had somehow discovered his birthday! His twenty-first birthday. Indeed, it was only proper that it be a grand event.

But it was just the Feast of the Conception of Saint Anne, the mother of the Blessed Virgin Mary, for Mary, being the mother of God, had been conceived without original sin. It had nothing to do with Don Giovanni's birthday. He should have known. Four years before, Emperor Manuel I Comnenus of Constantinople had declared this new holiday for the eastern branch of the church. The Greek population of Messina celebrated it, but not the Roman Catholics. In Palermo, though, everyone celebrated it, because the Norman royalty had taken a fancy to it.

Don Giovanni hadn't gone to the feast. Not because of his disappointment in its purpose, but because the man who issued the invitation quickly withdrew it upon meeting him face to face. Once people actually saw Don Giovanni, their reaction varied only in the degree of their rudeness. Some called him vile. Others gasped and covered their mouths before brutal words could burst out. None stayed to chat.

News spread rapidly, and only curiosity seekers came after that. Fewer all the time. No one at all had come this past week. Just as well: Don Giovanni didn't relish being a spectacle. The villa was quiet.

Today, Christmas, was particularly quiet. Don Giovanni had let his servants go home for the festivities. Right now the only other person in the villa was Ribi.

Having a home meant safety. Warmth. Having a cook meant regular meals of whatever he wanted.

What it didn't mean, though, was companionship. No one wanted to talk with Don Giovanni. No one came close. He wasn't even welcome in church in his present state.

But for Cani, he'd be entirely alone. The beggar boys didn't count; they didn't act like friends. How could they? You couldn't know someone you never talked with.

The courtyard air was frigid. Inside a fire played in the hearth. He could be in there. So why was he out here?

Storm clouds came. Even with his eyes closed, Don Giovanni could sense the darkening. He wasn't surprised. The sky had been dismal when he woke this morning. Yet he'd come out to the courtyard, anyway. Or maybe precisely because?

Rain.

It started as slow, heavy thumps. It drummed on his hands and through his thin rags of clothes. But on his head the beat was dulled by hair. He pushed his hair back until the rain met his bare forehead. He pressed on his facial hair until the rain laced his bare lips.

All summer long he had prayed for rain. Not in a conscious way. He never let himself actually think about warm water washing him from a benevolent sky. He knew that would make the act of being in the rain a violation of the wager terms. So he had cleared his mind and randomly chased the few storm clouds he saw, only to find, twice, that the brief rainfall had ceased by the time he got there.

Rain.

Sicily had plenty of it, but only in the winter. Summer rain was a phenomenon. That's why his mother used to celebrate it with a dance. Never had he understood her better. A bare-breasted dance.

Rain. Cold rain.

Now it turned icy. It came faster, pelting him.

Did he dare strip?

No, no. That would be too obvious.

Could he pull up his trousers and sleeves, at least?

He lay still, immobilized with fear and longing.

Had he known it would rain? Even though he'd kept his

mind from thinking about it, had some inner part of him known? Was he giving up? Losing the wager?

Cani whined.

Don Giovanni opened his eyes and pushed himself to a squat.

From every side sleet slashed like the thinnest knife blades.

Cani ran around and around Don Giovanni. He cried. He barked. Frantic eyes. Violent shivers. Poor dog. And it was Don Giovanni's fault.

"Sire. Sire, are you all right?" Ribi stood under the portico, wringing his hands. What an effort it must have been for the shy young man to address Don Giovanni directly. Everyone was suffering for him.

The sleet came so fast, it was hard to see now. Don Giovanni's rags stuck to his skin. The soaked mat of his hair weighed on his shoulders. The pounding outside his body was met by the pounding inside his head. He stretched his hands out and watched a small spot of clean skin appear on the back of one. An impossibility. A stranger born there. A miracle. The spot grew. Another appeared on the back of the other hand. Don Giovanni was there, under that dirt. He was there. He was the stranger. He still existed as a physical being in this world.

Cani ran under the portico and howled at him from that shelter. The dog shook so hard, his legs flew out from under him.

"Come out of the rain, sire," pleaded Ribi. "You'll catch your death of cold."

Was that what he was doing? Greeting death? Dying into damnation?

Don Giovanni got to his feet. He leaned forward and let the rain beat on his back and his buttocks. His rags stuck like a second skin now, particularly to the open sores. The dirt turned to mud under his feet. A puddle covered his toes. He pulled his hair up off his neck so the water ran in circles around and down his front. Let all the fetid rot go. Let it go, go, go. If this was the end of life, so be it. Off, damn dirt, damn filth. Off, off. Black passed before his eyes. He pressed his hands to his knees to steady himself, but the rain was too strong to stand up against. It buffetted him. It whipped him. In the end it beat him senseless.

He knew he was falling. He couldn't stop. He would die. He would lose.

The first thing he saw upon opening his eyes was Ribi, sitting against the wall, staring at him. The man's eyes registered terror. He was wet. Mud smeared across the front of his usually spotless smock and trousers.

"Did you carry me in from the courtyard on your own?" Don Giovanni's voice came out as a croak. "You're small. Did you drag me?"

"You're coherent again," Ribi said softly. "Good." His voice soothed. "Would you like me to help you out of those wet clothes?" His nostrils flared.

"You don't have to make an offer that disgusts you."

"I should have done it already." Ribi crawled forward. "You're shivering, despite the fire."

"No, no. You did right. Don't come closer. I can't take my clothes off. Never."

"Is that delirium speaking again?" Ribi perched back on his heels. "I should feel your head."

"Was I delirious before?" Don Giovanni sat up. "What did I say?"

"Things about the devil."

"What things?"

"Nonsense. Just nonsense. Are you feverish?"

"I don't think so." Don Giovanni had talked about the devil. But the devil wasn't here. Only Ribi was here. Maybe the devil had missed Don Giovanni's little attempt at cleanliness. Pathetic flirtation, given that he was now caked with mud. The devil's fire was narrowly avoided. Again. But this couldn't keep happening; the next time he would fall into the abyss. So there couldn't be a next time. "No, I'm not hot at all. I'm cold, Ribi. Rip down that tapestry and drape it over my back, would you?"

Ribi stood up and looked doubtfully at the wall. "That wall-hanging?"

"Yes."

"It's expensive."

"I hate it," said Don Giovanni. "Rip it down."

Ribi pulled on the tapestry hard. It came away easily, and he stumbled backward. He spread it over Don Giovanni's back.

"Thank you. Is the meal on the table?"

"Yes."

"Then go. Have a good holiday with your family."

"Are you . . . ?"

"Go."

"Thank you, sire." Ribi left.

Don Giovanni pulled the tapestry around himself and sidled over closer to the hearth. Gradually his shivers subsided. This ugly tapestry was good for something, after all. It lay so heavy across his shoulders that for the moment they didn't itch.

He got up and paced.

The boys didn't come home. Well, of course not. It was still sleeting. They'd stay in some public hall, dry. Singing. Drinking. Enjoying the company of friends—new friends, since their old ones resented their changed station in life. The boys were probably feasting. It didn't make sense for Don Giovanni to wait for them. He'd only be disappointed when they showed up already sated.

He sat at the table and ate neatly, with spoon and knife. Bowls of clove-scented water for washing fingers were set beside each plate. Polite people, of any class, kept their fingers clean when eating. Don Giovanni didn't use his bowl, naturally, but he was glad it was there. Ribi was a lucky find, a thoughtful soul to persist in putting the bowl there even when it wasn't touched. Someday Don Giovanni would use finger bowls again.

He would not lose.

He finished his meal, then walked through the villa. Don Muntifiuri had covered most of the walls in tapestries as ugly as the one wrapped around Don Giovanni now. This was a custom common in the northern lands he hailed from—Don Giovanni knew that. Still, nothing could justify them here in Sicily. They had turned moldy and musty in the humidity. Anyone could have predicted that. The entire villa had taken on a somberness in conflict with the joy of the Sicilian sun.

It was time for a change. Don Giovanni would give the place the exuberance that was its heritage by virtue of being built on this soil. He would refurbish the whole place. That's what he'd done when he'd taken over his castle in Messina. That's exactly what he should have started the very day he moved into this villa.

Oh yes, he would personally supervise all redecorating jobs, which he should start immediately with the new year. Tomorrow he'd get his servants to seek out artisans. He'd interview each personally.

But he wouldn't tell them to find only famous artisans. He'd put out the word that he was looking for new ideas. Any talented artist had a chance.

If there was one thing Don Giovanni understood it was that even the least likely characters deserved a chance to show their stuff.

Already his imagination was coloring the walls. Mosaics would be perfect. Little ceramic tiles, yes. But also lapis lazuli, jasper, and any other rare stones he wanted. And agate. Of course agate. Saint Agata must have been named for it. Maybe she loved it. Agate on the floors, on the walls. An eruption of jewels.

And the ceilings could be of honeycomb, with glimmers of gold. This villa would be more impressive than a cathedral. And more welcoming. Anyone who wanted Don Giovanni's company could enter.

Well, who would want his company? He wasn't a fool; he'd lost so much, but not his reason.

Still, he could pay for company. Not prostitutes—even the most desperate girl would refuse—but storytellers. Musicians. Theatrical groups.

The whole atmosphere of this place would change. His whole outlook on life, as well. This was a plan he could live with. The very sight of this villa would firm his resolve in moments of doubt.

He would not fall again.

He would not lose.

What Money Could Buy

"A LOAN?" DON GIOVANNI SAT ON A PILE OF CUSHIONS. IT WAS high, and gave the impression of grandness. The guest in front of him, the lawyer Don Cardiddu, sat on the floor, and Don Giovanni looked down on him from the soft pedestal. Like a king. The pomposity of the thought made him smile.

In actuality and, indeed, stark contrast, the cushions allowed him to rest without too much pain from the abscesses on his bottom. Hardly the backside of a king.

Or maybe exactly the appropriate backside for the king of rot. The little cloud of flies that had come with the summer's heat and circled his head right now could be his crown. Don Giovanni laughed.

Cani's head shot up. He'd been napping in the corner. He came over and sat near Don Giovanni's feet, looking at him expectantly. After all, Don Giovanni's laughter often led to a long sequence in which the man would chatter at the dog, who would whine appreciatively. It was a game the dog appeared to enjoy.

But Don Cardiddu had reacted differently. Worry crossed his face at that laugh. He took off his black hat and turned it around and around in his pudgy hands.

Don Giovanni stopped laughing. He didn't want the man to leave too quickly. It was so good to talk, no matter what the topic. He tried to look attentive. His face should welcome discourse.

Apparently it worked. Don Cardiddu gave a small smile. "Everyone knows of your wealth and your extreme generosity, how you give to the needy."

"The man you represent, though, he's not needy," said Don Giovanni, but kindly, "not if he uses your services."

"And that's why it's just a loan. He wants to build a magnificent villa on one of the hills to the east of Palermo, with fountains, baths, a small chapel with a cupola, a wonderful garden." Don Cardiddu got to his feet and walked to the window. He looked out on the courtyard. "You're doing a stunning job transforming this place. In what? Nine months of living here? You've made a great difference already."

All he'd done was pay for the work. The artists and artisans had done the rest. So many men, young and old, just waiting for a chance to show their talents. Each room of the villa was gradually taking on its own flavor; Don Giovanni had encouraged them to be innovative, and they hadn't hesitated. Did Don Cardiddu really appreciate the unusual quality of all this?

Don Cardiddu rested a hand on his fat belly. Don Giovanni could see only about a quarter of his profile, but it was enough. The lawyer had the figure of a squat woman, seven months pregnant. "I can imagine that courtyard with fountains at each corner."

So could Don Giovanni, but not until the wager was won. He wouldn't run the risk of clean water in his courtyard. Right now there was one fountain, at the northwest corner of the villa. He was careful never to walk past it.

"By the time you're through, it will be a palace," said Don Cardiddu. "It will rival the Castello di Mare Dolce of the king himself." He turned and nodded at Don Giovanni. "You can appreciate someone wanting this kind of thing."

"This kind of thing," echoed Don Giovanni thoughtfully. He climbed off his pile slowly and went to the wall. He ran his fingertips along the glassy, glossy surface. Enameled blue tiles ran from floor to ceiling. There was no design to them, just blue, walls of blue. In his head he called this the Wave Room. The great wave had started everything. He slept in this room.

The July sun was so bright, his reflection danced in the tiles. How very strange, since dancing was beyond him. He looked older, thinner, more haggard than his age. Anyone would have taken him for well past his prime. He put his hands flat on the reflection, blocking it. Then he turned and walked toward the door, with Cani at his heels.

Don Cardiddu quickly backed away, but not as much as he should have. No, for on this kind of day, in this kind of heat, Don Giovanni's odor reached far. Experience had taught him exactly how much distance people needed in which kinds of weather in order to be out of danger of gagging. The lawyer was trying not to show his revulsion. He was possibly a decent man. If only he would stay awhile.

Don Giovanni changed his mind and went, instead, through the opposite door into the next room, where a storyteller stood on a small stage before an audience of children. This was the Story Room. A never-ending string of storytellers intoned loudly on that stage, to a never-ending group of children during the day and adults in the evening. Anyone who wanted could come and listen to them. Anyone was welcome.

The stories were told in ordinary speech. A Sicilian that the common people could understand. Sometimes Arabic, but always the vernacular, not the literary form. Sometimes French.

Don Giovanni usually listened from behind the door, because the sight of him frightened new children, and adults, too. But now and then he longed to see the antics that went with the words, so he'd have a private storytelling session; just him alone in the far corner, with a storyteller on the stage. He might have a recitation in Greek then; it pleased his ears and was balm to his heart. Especially the poetry.

He passed quickly through the edge of the room now, noting the look of discomfort on Don Cardiddu's face at the sight of the ragtag children—which was precisely why he'd chosen this route, a little test for the man, who wasn't quite as decent as he could have been.

A boy caught a glimpse out of the corner of his eye, poked the boy beside him, and looked at Don Giovanni with huge eyes. Both of them pinched their noses.

Cani ran over and snuggled in with the children, a small group of whom now rolled around with the dog while others gaped at Don Giovanni, the bag of filth, the benevolent madman.

And Don Cardiddu was seeing all this. Seeing Don Giovanni's humiliation, which came at least daily, if not multiple times in a single day.

But it didn't matter. Children didn't know better. Don Giovanni didn't care. He couldn't let himself care.

He went down the stairs to the wine cellar with the lawyer following several steps behind. When he got to the bottom, he was disappointed to find that Cani had stayed with the children.

"Who would build it?" asked Don Giovanni.

Don Cardiddu jerked to attention, as though he'd forgotten why he'd come. "What do you mean?" he asked slowly. "Who would design the villa, is that what you mean?"

"No. Who would do the digging and the hauling and the stacking of stones?" Don Giovanni poured two glasses of wine and almost handed one to Don Cardiddu. Then he realized—of course—and left one glass on the side table, using a flick of his chin to invite the lawyer to help himself. He stepped back, allowing a wide berth. "Who would build it?"

Don Cardiddu looked confused. "The gentleman has a host of Arab slaves."

Don Giovanni sipped his wine. It was cool and fruity and perfect for this hot summer day.

Arab slaves. He thought of the beggar boy Kareem, whose name in Arabic meant "generous, noble." He hadn't seen much of him lately. The boy had opened up a stall in the Arab market square with a little help from Don Giovanni. He was doing fine, or so Zizu said.

"Who would use it?" asked Don Giovanni.

"His family, of course." Don Cardiddu picked up the glass, drank his wine, and set the empty glass back on the side table. He moved away again. "Have I not explained well?"

"You explained fine. More wine?"

"No, thank you."

Don Giovanni poured himself a second glass. "I won't loan him a single coin. Nothing."

Don Cardiddu's significant jowls went slack with disappointment, his belly drooped in resignation. He put on his hat.

"But if he frees his slaves and pays them a good wage, and if he opens the grounds as a public park, including the baths, I'll give him whatever it takes to build it. Not a loan—a gift. All of it." Don Giovanni finished his wine and poured himself a third glass. "Can you take him that message?"

Don Cardiddu blinked rapidly. He looked as if he might faint. "Free the slaves? He paid for them. Then give them a wage? That doesn't make sense. And it would cost him a great deal in the long run."

"Whatever it takes," said Don Giovanni. "I'll give whatever it takes. That makes it make sense."

Don Cardiddu seemed to catch his breath. "Yes. I see. Whatever it takes. I think, perhaps, that might be workable. That part, yes, I can take that idea to him. But having people he doesn't know in his private garden . . ."

"That's the point." Don Giovanni finished his wine. He poured himself a fourth glass. "It wouldn't be private. A public park."

"Who ever heard of such a thing?"

"They have them in Florence, on the mainland." Don Giovanni smiled at the lawyer. "You've heard of Florence, haven't you?"

Don Cardiddu came up to the table, reached for the jug, and poured himself a second glass of wine. He gulped it down. He stood closer to Don Giovanni than anyone had in a long time.

"Remember how you told Don Muntifiuri not to act like a fool?" said Don Giovanni in hardly more than a whisper. He must do nothing to make the man move away, no loud noise, no sudden movement, barely a breath. "Do the same service to your new client. Make him see the sense of it. This villa he wants to build is already going to be up in the hills. Not that many people will come all the way out there, and not very often. But whoever comes must be allowed to pass unmolested." He smiled in what he hoped was a winning way. "Whatever it takes." He bowed.

"I'll relay the message."

"And the baths must be open to the public. Make sure you tell him that. The baths must be included in the deal."

Don Cardiddu left.

The man had been close. Don Giovanni had nearly touched him.

"Nice of you to visit," he said to the empty space.

"It's always a pleasure," he answered.

He had talked to himself. Had he done that before? Well, talking to himself didn't mean anything. He wasn't crazy, he was simply lonely.

He poured himself another glass of wine and drank it down. Inebriation offered a buffer against reality. He kissed the edge of the glass. He drank directly from the jug and kissed it, too. He got on his knees and kissed the stone floor.

Then he walked outside under the portico that surrounded the courtyard, keeping well in the shade. From the dining hall upstairs the voices of children eating lunch wafted down. Anyone who came to Don Giovanni's home could have a hearty meal, whatever time of day. Ribi ran a kitchen staff of several. Don Giovanni didn't even know how many. It didn't matter; the purse never let him down.

And anyone who wanted could have a bed for the night. Don Giovanni had added two very large halls to ensure that no one would ever be turned away.

It was a life. He was managing.

A bark came. A joyful yip, really. And laughter. Cani was obviously having lunch with the children and enjoying himself as much as they were. He was probably under the table, eating from little hands that offered treats. Licking little toes. Nosing little bellies. Don Giovanni had seen Cani do these things before.

He'd be hungry right now, too, if it weren't for that wine. Hungry, but not able to join the crowd in the dining hall. He was perhaps the only soul in Palermo not welcome at his own table.

His heart beat jaggedly. *Bum, ba ba bum.* It beat inside his head. *Bum, ba ba bum.* Louder. Deafeningly loud. Sweat broke out on his forehead, back, chest. It drenched him in a flood, everywhere. Not from the heat of the day. Not something innocuous. This was his personal source of sweat. This sweat came with the irregular beat of his heart drum.

That man, that client of Don Cardiddu's, would accept the offer. He'd have to be an idiot not to. There would be a public park in the eastern hills, with a public bath. Everyone could be clean. Everyone but Don Giovanni.

Bum, ba ba bum.

What was cleanliness, anyway? The whole of nature was dirty, after all. What could be wrong with dirt?

Yet Cani kept himself clean. Even bees washed their faces. Don Giovanni had watched them. Enviously.

Anything that could manage it wanted to stay clean. That was the rule. Don Giovanni went against the rule.

Cleanliness was organization. And organization of the body freed the mind and spirit.

Freedom. Money could buy a slave freedom, but no amount of money could free Don Giovanni.

Sweat dripped into his eyes and stung. Cleansing sweat. If only he could be truly bathed in it.

Water, water. Oh, the holiness of water.

A flash of realization made Don Giovanni spasm. The lack of cleanliness was an invitation to decay. That's what made it horrific. That's why people hated it. It wasn't just that they didn't understand why he wouldn't clean himself, or that they took it as a sign of disrespect for all they valued. It was that his filth reminded them of their own mortality. That's why they hated him. Don Giovanni was a testament to each of them, each person he passed: You, too, will die.

Bum, ba ba bum.

Crazy heartbeat. And dripping sweat. And the wave of nausea, the sick rise in his throat, that was part of it, too. This had happened before. Ugly syndrome. Bile filled his mouth. He knew it would. Breath came fast and shallow and faster and more shallow. He couldn't catch it. He couldn't breathe. He'd die. He'd die right here in the courtyard and no one would want to handle his disgusting corpse.

Evan Cani would hold back. He'd seen the dog's habits. The woods south of the villa were Cani's favorite playground, and he'd walked with the dog there many times. Cani would kill a rabbit and chew its flesh, hot blood running down his jaw, marrow smeared in his muzzle hairs. But he'd sniff at a rotting carcass that had been baking in the sun and walk away.

Nothing good could come now. Nothing good could ever happen.

Panic brought him to his knees. Like in the wine cellar. But he didn't kiss the floor this time. No one would ever want his kisses. Maybe even the stone of the wine cellar had cringed, and he was just too blind and stupid to understand. No one, nothing wanted his kisses. No one, nothing would ever kiss him again. He'd die unkissed, unloved.

How unutterably stupid he had been to enter into this wager. How devoid of understanding.

Nothing good. Ever again.

Only dread.

A Gift

ON ALL SAINTS' AND ALL SOULS' DAY OF 1171, DON GIOVANNI GAVE the biggest feast Sicily had ever heard of. He sent out criers saying everyone was welcome—no matter what their station in life.

The poor came from all over the northwest of the island. Most of the weavers of Palermo were busy for the month of October making blankets for these visitors, so that they could sleep comfortably. Most of the potters were busy making amphoras and dishes and cups. Straw mats, a full hand's thickness, covered the floors of all the rooms that would be used as dormitories. Ribi hired dozens of extra helpers. The villa buzzed like a beehive.

The food was meant to please everyone. There was minestrone with only vegetables, and minestrone with sausage chunks. Breads in the shape of crosses piled high in the center of the courtyard tables. *Arancine*—fried rice balls stuffed with cheese and peas—and *caponata*—eggplant, onion, and pepper stew—and boiled octopus, raw sea urchins, steamed fish, and grilled pork intestines. Platters overflowed with braised boar, lamb, goat. Pies of nightingales, braces of stuffed peacocks, roasted crane and heron. The food of kings. But peasant food wasn't overlooked, either; there were batter-fried greens, fennel dipped in garlic and anchovies, artichokes stuffed with bread and cheese, *frittate*—omelets—with grated goat cheese. Local apples and grapes sat beside pears brought all the way from Mount Etna.

And sweets—it seemed Ribi knew how to make every pastry imaginable, many dripping with honey and rose water, smothered in pistachios and cinnamon. Cream puffs ringed huge bowls of ices. Snow had not yet fallen on Monte Pellegrino to the west, so Don Giovanni had sent people inland for it. They'd finally found the first snow of the season on a plain midway up to the mountain town of Corleone, directly south of Palermo. They'd had to hard-pack huge quantities of it, in order to have enough not melt by the time of the feast. The ices were flavored with mulberries, figs, apricots, lemon, coffee, almond.

Almond was always a favorite in sweets. Almond cookies, pastries, cakes. But the crown of almond desserts—*marzapane*—was Ribi's specialty. It was important not to use shelled, dried almonds; they didn't hold enough oil. So in the last days before the festival Ribi's helpers broke fresh almonds with hammers, peeled the kernels, then ground them in a mortar, gradually adding rose water and sugar to make a thick, aromatic paste. They kneaded it, pressed it with stone rollers, folded it, and pressed again, over and over, until the paste was fine and smooth.

Most cooks shaped the paste into simple forms, typically flat coins. But Ribi's recipe had egg white, and that gave the paste a stiffness that would hold. He divided the paste into many bowls and added fruit and vegetable juices to color them blue and purple and green, red and yellow and orange. He modeled them into little fruits and hung them from silver strings dangling off the eaves of the courtyard portico. He said he'd learned the trick from nuns at a convent in the hills, famous for their *cassate*—cakes made from *marzapane*, ricotta, and candied fruit. He made those cakes, too.

Don Giovanni looked out at the festivities from behind the curtains that he had hung over the Wave Room windows just for this occasion. That way he could see everyone's merrymaking without the sight of him disrupting it.

Not a soul didn't lie back happy and satiated that night. Not a soul didn't sleep in peace.

Not even Don Giovanni. He'd passed most of the autumn in a drunken haze. But Zizu kept checking up on him throughout the festival to make sure he didn't drink himself into oblivion. The boy would simply pick up the jug Don Giovanni was reaching for and carry it away. He'd have to wait for a servant to come along before he could ask for another jug. And soon after it would arrive, Zizu would be back to snatch it away. When Don Giovanni asked him what he was doing, the boy said he was protecting Don Giovanni's right to enjoy the day. Just like that.

Somehow the boy had come to care about him.

That startling and blessèd realization alone would have made Don Giovanni sleep exceptionally well. But seeing clear-eyed the pleasure he was giving everyone helped, too.

Sleep allowed escape. Usually.

Sometimes nightmares would come. The worst were exactly like his waking hours. If they came two nights in succession, he had a fail-safe remedy. He'd drink in the evening until he passed out. It broke the nightmare cycle every time.

He woke the morning after the festivities intoning the date inside his head: 2 November 1171. One year, three months, and two days to go. He closed himself in the Wave Room and poured a glass of red wine from the jug that was always waiting there. He could endure that period. So long as he had his wine.

On the western edge of Sicily, in the north, lay the city of Trapani. Uphill from it was the small town of Erice. After sampling wines from every producer of reasonable size in the entire island of Sicily over the past year, Don Giovanni had developed a taste for wines from Erice. They were less sweet than the wines from Marsala, and not as robust as those from the east coast, near Messina. Appreciating their delicacy made him feel refined again, so long as he drank them in solitude. If another person passed him as he was drinking, their reaction to the sight of him would inevitably destroy the illusion, because no one could hide their disgust. Not even Zizu. Not even Ribi. It might be a slight shift of the eyes, or a flare of the nostrils, but it was there. Always.

Slow sips were best. The red liquid slid over his tongue and warmed his throat as it went down. A second glass. A third. More. He lost count. He was still drinking from the glass, not from the jug, so it couldn't be that many. Not yet.

He went to the dining hall. Everyone else had already eaten, so it was his turn. Big yellow fluted mushrooms fried in olive oil sat on a platter in the center of the table. Zizu must have collected them this morning. They used to be Don Giovanni's favorite, but they didn't interest him anymore. None of it interested him, really.

He walked around the table, letting his fingers do the grazing. A little here, a little there. Cani joined him. Don Giovanni fed the dog from his fingers, then ate from them himself. What did it matter?

"What do you think about the problems in Turkey?" he said to the air.

"Turkey? No one talks to me about that."

"Of course not. But if they understood you could solve whatever money can solve, they'd talk to you."

"What can money solve?"

Ah, that was the real question.

He was talking to himself again. Cani didn't look alarmed. Why should he? Talking to yourself was not problematic in its own right. It was when you thought you heard voices that you were verifiably crazy. Or maybe not. You might just be an idiot. Or a saint.

This part of the day seemed irrelevant to Don Giovanni. He tasted nothing by now, because the wine had already done its lovely, reliable job on his senses. But Ribi insisted he eat food at least twice a day. So he did, just to keep the man from nagging. And because, of course, he knew Ribi was right: physical degradation led to mental degradation.

Someday he'd reward Ribi for this insistence. Maybe with an inn of his own, where people could come from all over to taste the food of the grand chef. But not now. "For now," said Don Giovanni to the air, "for now I need you here."

"Who, sire? Yourself? Is that who you need here?"

Don Giovanni turned. Standing against the wall was a small figure dressed in loose black trousers, a long black smock, and a black wool cap. He was slighter even than Ribi. And very young; no hair grew on his face yet. His jawline was delicate. Effeminate. And his luminous gray eyes blinked just once, then steadied on Don Giovanni. Beside him on the floor was a wooden box.

Was he vision or reality? "Have we met?"

"Twice."

Don Giovanni shook his head. He'd encountered the devil three times, not two. Still, it had been a long while since the last visit—the devil was due. Overdue. He had to keep an eye on his wager, after all. "Are you poor at numbers?"

The boy's face stayed pleasant. "Probably no worse than most artists. You hired me to paint the library." He lowered his head a little and gave a small, apologetic smile. "It was long ago. And you were hiring many people at once."

Don Giovanni wished he hadn't drunk those last few glasses of wine. A clear head would serve him now, for he was almost sure the boy was real.

So this was the hand that had painted fronds and clouds and stony outcroppings with little bits of animals poking out from behind, just enough that even children could guess at what was hidden there. He knew, because he'd watched them stand and study, then shriek in delight. He'd thought it a strange choice for a library at first, but the children had made him recognize how appropriate it was. It piqued the imagination, just as a good book did. "You said twice?"

The boy cleared his throat. "Last week you hired me to paint the columns of the portico for All Saints' and All Souls' Day."

"That wasn't long ago."

"But you were hiring so many more," said the boy.

"Ribi did much of the hiring."

"Still, the confusion . . ."

"Why are you making excuses for me?"

"I don't know. I apologize."

Don Giovanni felt breathless, the exchange had gone so quickly. He looked at the box on the floor. "What's that?"

"I thought you might want a drawing."

"There's a drawing in the box?"

"The things to make a drawing are in there."

"You want to make me a drawing? Of what?"

"Yourself. A portrait."

Don Giovanni's heart stopped. It took all his energy not to fall back a step, not to stagger under the blow. How could a face that looked as harmless as this boy's belong to so cruel a soul? "Why would I want a portrait?"

"You talk to yourself."

"Many people do."

"You seem lonely. I thought if you had a portrait to talk to . . ."

"Why a portrait of myself? Why not a portrait of the king? Shouldn't I be addressing the king? Don't I merit that? Or a beautiful woman. Voluptuous. Seductive. Don't I merit that?" Don Giovanni realized he was shouting.

The boy stood looking at him. His breath came so hard his shoulders actually rose and fell. But his gaze was clear. Unwavering.

Fear rolled through Don Giovanni. It pressed on him, from the inside toward the outside. What would a portrait reveal?

Did he dare face it? A sense of inevitability grew over him like a second skin. "Are you waiting for an invitation?"

The boy shook his head. He quickly kneeled and opened the box. He took out a charcoal and a rolled-up piece of papyrus.

Pathetic. "You needed a whole box just for that?"

The boy licked his bottom lip. "There are other things in the box."

Don Giovanni walked forward slowly, fighting nervous spasms in his chest.

The boy didn't get up from his knees, but he didn't cower, either. That was surprising, given how weak he seemed. Even his voice was nothing but a slender reed.

Don Giovanni stared down into the box. "You have paints in there. And vellum. Don't I merit those better materials?"

"The papyrus comes from near Siracusa. It's the highest quality. And it's better for charcoal. I thought maybe a quick sketch to get started. So we can both get more at ease."

"Both? You may not be at ease, I can understand that. But this is my home. I'm master here. I'd call this a bad start."

The boy stood. The top of his head barely came to Don Giovanni's lips, but he looked into Don Giovanni's face with . . . what? Defiance? "Where do you want to sit?"

"How many portraits have you done?"

The boy put one finger to his cheek. "Let me count. Hmmm. Thousands? Or is that just evidence of my poor numbers?" His eyes teased. They actually teased. "Look, you chose me for the library. You chose me for the columns. Does any other credential matter?" He licked his bottom lip again. "Where do you want to sit?"

"No one will ever love me again." Don Giovanni's mouth dropped open. He breathed like a dog. The words in his head had come without bidding, almost a reaction to the proximity of this boy. How disturbing. But, worse, he was half sure he'd heard them. And the boy had blanched. "Did I just speak?"

The boy pressed his lips together so hard, they went white. But he kept his eyes steady on Don Giovanni.

"Tell me. Did I just say that out loud?"

"You have a nice voice."

"Do you mean that?"

"Yes."

"I can't remember . . . I don't always think straight these days, you see. But maybe this is the first time in two years that someone has found something about my physical self pleasing. Someone other than Cani. He's my dog."

"Not so bad a start then, after all." The boy gave a small smile. "Where do you want to sit?"

"Did you say my voice was nice just to make a better start?"

"Yes. But it's true. Where do you want to sit?"

"You're persistent."

"It's one of my more annoying traits, according to my mother."

"Do you always listen to your mother?"

"Don't you?"

"My mother died when I was thirteen."

"I'm sorry. My father died when I was eleven."

"My father died when I was thirteen."

"I guess you've got me beat. Where do you want to sit?"

Don Giovanni smiled. "Can you tell I'm smiling?"

"Yes."

"But there's all this dirty hair hanging over my lips."

"Your eyes show."

This artist boy was intriguing. Or maybe not. Maybe he was just ordinary and Don Giovanni was so starved for real conversation that he'd find a half-wit charming. "I'll have pity on you. Let's take blankets and wrap up tight and sit in the courtyard. That way you won't pass out from my odors." There. Let the boy mutter some stupid contradiction about how the odors weren't that bad. Or maybe he'd even deny them altogether. Just how insincere could he be?

"Thank you. Lead the way."

"I like you." The words came out on their own.

"Good."

"Why? Why is that good?" Are you going to say you like me, too? When do the lies start?

"I'm slow at drawing, so we'll have to spend a lot of time together. It'll be easier if you like me."

An honesty that would be scathing, he was sure, in other contexts. But, oh, oh no, he saw the trick. He'd been right in his first guess. "Do you like dogs? What I mean is, are you the devil?"

"Yes. And no. Are you Muslim?"

"Why would you ask such a thing?"

"Why would you put together liking dogs with being the devil?"

"Actually, I put not liking dogs with being the devil."

"That's even less explicable."

"You talk like a refined person."

"So do you."

"Do you really like dogs?"

"Yes. I like most animals." The boy scratched the side of his nose. His hands were small. "Especially birds."

"I haven't had this long a conversation with anyone in over two years."

"This is the second time you've talked about the past two years. What happened? What made them different?"

"It started with a huge wave. It came over the walls of Messina."

"Then you're wrong. It started with an eruption of Mount Etna. And it was almost three years ago. I remember. Catania was leveled by the earthquake that followed and Messina was half washed away. Everyone talked about it. My mother wished my father were still alive to help figure out what to do about it. People here are glad they don't live under the threat of the fire mountain."

The image of Randazzo's streets black with ash made Don Giovanni close his eyes. But then he thought of spring on the mountain. "It's hard to understand living like that. But a few things help."

"A few things?"

"Butterflies. Yellow butterflies. Do you understand me?"

"I'm trying to."

"Why?"

"It's the natural thing people do, don't you think?"

"No one's been natural around me . . ."

"For the past two years." The boy smiled winningly as he finished Don Giovanni's sentence. "Or should I correct that to three?"

"No. It was two. You're right about the date of the wave. But my demise, shall we say, started later that year. On All Saints' and All Souls' Day."

"Then almost exactly two years ago. Not my favorite holiday. Saint stories give me the creeps."

"You don't like the image of severed parts on silver platters?"

"You're talking about Saint Agata. I hate her story most of all. So what happened on All Saints' and All Souls' Day two years ago?"

"I don't know if I can tell you."

"That's all right. I didn't mean to pry."

"No, what I mean is that I don't know if it's within the rules of the game to tell."

"What game?"

"It's a wager, actually."

"I don't like gambling myself."

"Do you lack faith?"

The artist blinked. "I don't understand the connection."

"Maybe there isn't one. I debate it with myself now and then. You didn't answer my question."

"My faith is in my art. Shall we begin?"

Don Giovanni led the way out to the courtyard, calling to Zizu for blankets.

They sat in the weak sun and cold air and talked of this and that while the boy drew. Don Giovanni changed positions often, always trying to escape putting too much pressure on sore spots. But the artist never complained. He didn't demand that his subject be still.

Ribi brought them the midday meal in a basket, because the boy preferred to eat with Don Giovanni rather than join the others at the dining table. The boy carefully carried the easel and all his art materials inside to the Wave Room. Then he came back outside and held the basket in one hand and they walked with Cani through the fields, eating and talking. The boy admitted he felt daring to eat as he stood, holding the food in one hand, licking his fingers. Daring. Like Don Giovanni had felt back in his castle, the morning after the wave. A memory of irrecoverable habits, someone else's life.

They lost track of time and walked the whole afternoon. Don Giovanni's feet went numb from the cold, but he didn't care. Conversation warmed him in places that he'd thought were frozen permanently.

When the light began to fade, they returned to the villa. Don Giovanni stood in the doorway of the Wave Room and for a moment it seemed the universe had gone silent. He felt like they'd arrived at the moment of truth, which was absurd. This was just a young boy, inexperienced at both art and life. What did it matter? Yet his voice still had a tremolo when he asked, "Can I see what you drew?"

The artist handed the papyrus to him.

The page was a dark smear. A mess, really. But under the smear he could make out the ragged form of a man, whose hands moved high, by his face. The more he looked at them, the more the hands took form, until they were the only clear things on the page. They seemed to fly. And not wildly—not bashing. Gracefully.

"They're birds."

Don Giovanni looked around in surprise. Zizu had entered the room without a sound. It was Zizu who had spoken.

"You mean his hands?" asked the artist.

"Yes." Zizu studied the drawing. "You did them good. Good hands."

Don Giovanni remembered standing in his castle window thinking of birds—of how birds indoors were bad luck. But these birds were outside. They'd been in the courtyard, after all. These birds were free. "Zizu's right," said Don Giovanni. "Wonderful birds."

"So you're pleased?"

He was. "How much do you want for this?"

"It's an initial sketch. The portrait will be better."

"I don't want a portrait. I want this."

"All right then, it's yours."

"How much?"

"Nothing."

"A gift?"

"Something so simple isn't worthy of the title of gift."

"I deem it worthy."

The boy smiled. "All right, then I bestow upon you this magnificent gift, sire." He bowed, and so deeply Don Giovanni thought his nose might graze the floor.

Supplicants

THE NEXT MORNING DON GIOVANNI WALKED THROUGH HIS villa, every single room. The boy artist was nowhere to be found. Well, of course. His job was finished. Don Giovanni had stupidly told him the drawing was enough, so he hadn't returned. All right, then he'd have to find another job for him. The ceilings could be redone again. All of them.

He called in Ribi and told him to fetch the boy. But Ribi had no idea where to find him. In the past the boy artist had come to Don Giovanni's villa on his own, in response to the criers' calls announcing the need for artists.

So Don Giovanni had criers sent out again; artists swarmed his villa again. But not the artist Don Giovanni was seeking.

Not his friend. That's what the boy was. A human friend. Found and lost in a single day. And Don Giovanni hadn't even asked his name. How stupid and thoughtless could he have been?

The interrogations began. Ribi called in everyone he had hired in the week before All Saints' and All Souls' Day. Don Giovanni questioned each thoroughly. Most didn't remember the quiet artist. Those who did had no idea who he was, where he came from. Not even the other artists knew his identity.

How could finding one willow switch of a boy be that hard? After all Don Giovanni had been through, this particular challenge should have been nothing.

He had Zizu organize a troop of beggar boys to fan out across all of Palermo to find the boy. When that failed, he paid Don Cardiddu to send out messengers all over northwestern Sicily. They'd find the boy. They'd bring him back to Don Giovanni like a gift—a Christmas gift by now.

Christmas passed. The New Year came. No luck.

Don Giovanni stopped the search. He closed himself in the Wave Room and took out the sketch he conversed with every morning. "It's worse now, isn't it?"

"Far worse," the sketch answered. "The boy crystallized the pain."

"I am alone."

"You don't have to be. The lines are long. Ever since you funded that public park. Open the doors and in they come."

"Being with them is the most isolating of all."

"I know."

"But it gives structure to the day."

"I know."

"So I have to tell Don Cardiddu I'll open the doors."

The sketch didn't answer.

The next day Don Giovanni carefully, oh so carefully, settled himself into the cushions in the Wave Room. Wine dulled pain so well—the breakfast of choice was once more his. He'd given it up during his search for the boy artist because he wanted a clear head. Now the last thing he wanted was a clear head.

This room was a fine place to wait.

But he didn't have to wait long. A servant came in and held palm fronds in front of Don Giovanni, to screen him from view. Another servant led in the first guest.

Guest? More like supplicant. From then on they came in a steady succession and sat on a bench by the window, so that the breeze blew from them toward Don Giovanni and not vice versa. Sitting, they were on eye level with him, but they typically kept their eyes on the floor, like one averts the gaze from the blinding sun. They didn't try to catch a glimpse of him behind the palm frond.

Could an ugly sight actually hurt the eyes?

But it was boring to pose such questions. It was boring to feel sorry for himself.

He remembered the devil talking of boredom. In fact, the devil had offered the wager to assuage his boredom with the ordinary open swap. Boredom could lead to evil.

It was better to think instead of what he could still do with his day. He was a benefactor; and that was far from boring. There were judgments to be made. Giving had its dangers. It could ruin motivation and lead to slovenliness and pointlessness. It could give one man an unfair advantage, causing harm to others. Remarkably, denial was as much a responsibility as assent.

That's why Don Giovanni didn't get really drunk until evening.

Time slugged along. Somewhere in there, his twenty-second birthday passed. He refused to think about it. Who cared that he'd been born?

Public parks sprang up throughout the region as men who wanted to build new villas decided a park on their grounds was worth the relief from building costs. Public baths became ubiquitous. Innkeepers financed expansions of their businesses by agreeing to build rooms on the bottom floors where the indigent could stay—with free meals. Practically overnight, beggars disappeared from the streets of Palermo. Freed slaves did much of the new building going on, but for wages now.

And through all this, snow showers gave way to spring rains then heat waves then just plain broiling sun.

The hotter it got, the more the fungus and insects thrived and multiplied on Don Giovanni's body. He hated them. Zizu made him a salve from a plant that grew white flowers. It helped with the itching and the occasional sting, but it didn't kill them.

Just as well, Don Giovanni told himself, for he had now taken to talking to them. The sketch was still his morning greeting; he could no longer imagine starting the day without it. But he didn't carry it around with him for fear of damaging or even losing it. Bugs, however, bugs were constant companions.

He slept on piles of rose petals now. That was Zizu's idea. The boy thought the sweet scent would benefit all. He was a heartfelt child. But wrong. Sweet rot was just as revolting to humans as sour rot. Still, an unexpected advantage came from the flower petals. When Don Giovanni's smock and trouser legs rode up, a velvety bandage would stick to a festering boil. Sometimes he was lucky and the petal protected the wound long enough for a scab to form. When it fell off, he was minus one source of misery.

So he carefully covered the remaining ones with velvet petals. As summer progressed, the roses faded. His servants went out into the woods to collect wildflowers for his bed. Not all of those flowers worked like roses. But when autumn came to the pine groves, the men found dainty blossoms that ranged from pink to deep wine color with thick, glossy petals—those worked almost as well as roses. By October, all his pustules were gone, except the ones under his hair.

October. From the very first of the month, everyone talked about the coming festivities again. Everyone knew All Saints' and All Souls' Day was important to Don Giovanni. The whole of Palermo got involved in the preparations.

It was the second week of October when a very different sort of man visited Don Giovanni. He brushed aside the servants and strode into the room in expensive, stylish clothes, with a wide-rimmed black hat that resembled a clergyman's. He practically clicked together the heels of his black boots as he stood in front of the bench, rather than sitting like the others. "Could I speak with you in private, sire?"

The very request made Don Giovanni's skin tighten in excitement. "Yes."

The servant who held the palms that screened him from sight questioned with his eyes. Then he bowed in obedience and left.

Don Giovanni was alone with a stranger. And the stranger didn't blanch. Instead, he looked down on him steadily, even as he bowed, touching the edge of his hat in a gesture of respect.

"I am a messenger. I bring a request from King William."

Don Giovanni had to catch his breath. He remembered talking to the boy artist, haughtily saying he merited conversation with the king. It was a bitter joke then; no king would stoop so low. But now here was a messenger. It thrilled him. He had met the young king only four years before—but it might as well have been a lifetime ago. William had been timid, though a likeable enough boy, and generous with his harem. "How can I serve my king?"

"As you know, King William is of age."

There had been a gigantic party. Nobles came from as far

away as England to celebrate the eighteenth birthday of the king. Don Giovanni had managed to glean only the vaguest bits of information about it. And that had been quite a while ago now, so how could a brain fogged by wine be expected to hold on to such things for so long? One detail he did remember, though: he had not been invited. "Yes?"

"It's time for him to establish himself."

"He's king. What more establishing does he need?"

The messenger smiled. "Rightly said. But he was only thirteen when his father died. That leaves a boy vulnerable and, to some extent, weak."

Don Giovanni had been only thirteen when both his parents died. "He has a mother," he said coolly.

"The dear Queen Margaret." The messenger's tone said it all.

And Don Giovanni knew the story, at least up to the moment when the wave hit Messina, the moment when he left polite society. After her husband's death, Queen Margaret had ruled at first through Peter, a Saracen eunuch freed by King William I. But so many barons pitted themselves against Peter, he ran off to Morocco. Her cousin Stephen ran things for a couple of years then, but he stole money away to France and when people heard about that, there were riots in the streets. Messina certainly had its share of them. Stephen fled to Jerusalem. Then the Englishman Walter had come on the scene, somehow getting the queen to rely on him. The last Don Giovanni knew, this

Walter had riled the Palermo mob into forcing the canons to elect him archbishop. That was right before the wave.

Since then, whatever had happened to the royal family was a mystery to Don Giovanni. But he sensed that if he let this messenger realize the extent of his ignorance, he'd reduce his ability to negotiate whatever was to come. So he sighed, knowingly.

"Queen Margaret did her best," said the messenger tiredly, as though agreeing with Don Giovanni's sigh. "But a tutor can have more influence over a youth than is healthy. Especially a zealously pious tutor like Archbishop Walter. To become a man, sometimes a youth needs to throw off the shackles of his tutor."

Don Giovanni thought of old Don Alfinu; no one could be more self-righteously pious than him. "I understand what it means to throw off those kinds of shackles." He stood. "Would you like a glass of wine? It's from the best cellar in Erice." Had he spoken too spontaneously? He looked quickly at the side table. Fortunately, Ribi had placed a fresh glass beside the jug. Don Giovanni motioned with one hand. "Please help yourself."

The messenger went straight to the table and poured a full glass. He knew how to act friendly to a drunk, at least.

"What is King William's plan?" asked Don Giovanni.

"He wants to build a cathedral."

Don Giovanni laughed. "That hardly seems a way to demonstrate independence from the archbishop."

"Oh, but it is. A very clever way." The messenger sipped his wine. He nodded in appreciation. "He's going to build the most magnificent cathedral ever. It will have two massive bell towers. The famous bronze sculptor Bonanno of Pisa will make doors with bas-reliefs from the Old and New Testaments. There will be a wide central nave with two smaller naves flanking. And granite columns, eighteen of them, supporting pointed arches." One hand drew the arches in the air as he spoke. "In the Arab style. The roof will be carved meticulously and painted lushly. The floor will be white marble from Taormina. Mosaics will run from floor to ceiling." He shook his head. "Can you think of a better way to show the archbishop that you're in control, even on his turf?"

Put that way, it was smart. Don Giovanni hadn't caught that in the boy he'd met years ago. But then, boys changed. Don Giovanni had.

"Such a cathedral will take years to build."

The messenger finished his wine and put the glass back on the side table. "Decades."

"And lots of gold," said Don Giovanni.

"Exactly. King William wants to start the work when he turns twenty-one, in 1174, only a year and a half from now. He needs to raise funds."

"Where will the cathedral be?" asked Don Giovanni.

"In Monreale."

Don Giovanni had been to Monreale. It was on a hillside to the southwest of Palermo, and it looked down on the most stunning bay. "That's a little Arab town. Why place a cathedral there?"

"To make another point. King William is justly tolerant of everyone—Jews, Muslims, and Greek Orthodox Catholics. But he wants to let the world know that Sicily accepts the Roman Catholic Church as its official church. He's a papist."

Some papist. "What about his harem?"

The messenger gave that knowing smile again. "Recognizing the fundamental laws of the kingdom doesn't require slavish obedience. And asceticism doesn't befit a king. Wouldn't you agree?"

Asceticism. Not having a harem would amount to asceticism to this young king. What Don Giovanni wouldn't give for just one woman's kiss.

He couldn't think about this. And it didn't matter anyway whether or not he agreed with the young king's ideas on asceticism. He would contribute to this symbol of independence. He had decided that when he'd offered the messenger wine. "Where is the king now?"

"At the Castello di Mare Dolce, near the port of Palermo."

"Fine," said Don Giovanni. "Please tell him to expect a delivery tomorrow."

"Magnificent. That's what everyone says you are. They're right."

A sensation of lightness enveloped Don Giovanni. He felt himself to be a mass of minuscule pieces, just barely clinging together.

Pride

THAT AFTERNOON DON GIOVANNI HAD HIS SERVANTS BUY enormous wagons. In the morning the Wave Room was full of gold. The servants shoveled it into sacks, which they piled high in the wagons. They went along the coastal road in file, to deliver the precious load to the castle.

Don Giovanni stood at the Wave Room window and watched long after they were out of sight. He had not asked for a single concession. He gave the money without conditions.

Still, something significant had happened. The king of all Sicily had turned to Don Giovanni for help. Yes, it was just money, and by this point Don Giovanni knew very well the limitations of wealth. But it was a start. If the king could only come to rely on his aid, Don Giovanni had a chance to influence him in other ways. He could reshape how the court did things. And since the rich of Sicily looked to the king as their model, he could reshape the habits of the nobility all across the island. He could make this land a kinder place, a serene place, where everyone had a bed, and everyone went to it with a full belly.

A new realization came: People with full bellies had fewer reasons to do others harm. Oh yes, Don Giovanni could make this wager the most expensive one the devil had ever entered. He could make it worth having endured all of this.

The first of November was less than two weeks away. All Saints' and All Souls' Day. The third anniversary of the wager.

The taste of winning made Don Giovanni's tongue tip curl slightly upward. In that very moment the urge to urinate came swiftly, without warning. He wet himself. How horrifying. In all the time that he'd been dirty, he'd never wet or soiled himself after that one time on the road outside Randazzo when the thieves had beaten him brutally. He was filthy, yes, but none of it was his fault. Until now. He had to fight the need to rip off his clothes.

To add insult to injury, it stung. Not just the urine against his skin. This was a sharp bite in the end of his member. He'd put up with lice and grime in his most private places, but now an abscess. No!

He took the ever-present jug of wine and splashed it down the front of his pants. It was better to smell like a besotted drunk than a sack of urine. No one should know what had happened. No one.

He'd wet himself. The thought was maddening. He needed diversion. Ribi could be counted on to help get his mind somewhere else.

There would be another grand feast on the holiday, of course. Bigger this year, because the word had spread farther. Preparations for housing all the guests had begun in early September. Everyone had been bustling around him ever since. Now and then a servant would ask his opinion on some decision. But generally it all happened independently of him. He was the source of money, that's all. Ribi and the servants did the rest.

Another realization came: the boy artist was sure to know artists were needed here again. He'd come last year, after all. And no matter how far he may have traveled in the interim, he'd have heard that this year's celebration would be grander. He might come seeking employment again. He could. He very well could.

A tentative but oh-so-sweet hint of optimism accompanied Don Giovanni to the kitchen. He nestled into his favorite corner to watch. Already calm was returning. He could bear the insult of that little incident with the urine. The kitchen was a good place.

Ribi took a round wooden board from a shelf and cut small wedges from several different kinds of soft cheeses. He arranged them on the board and held it out to Don Giovanni. These were not ordinary cheeses. Some had dried fruits pressed into them; others had assorted nuts or a variety of salted meats. Many were flavored with alcoholic drinks. Ribi made the choices of which things to blend into which cheeses. It was his invention. Nowhere else in Sicily would you taste such things.

Don Giovanni ate one. Walnut with ricotta soured by lemon. Odd and zingy and altogether delightful. And so simple, really. Nothing exotic or difficult to work with. "A touch of genius," he said.

Ribi grinned.

The urge came immediately. Don Giovanni turned his back in the nick of time. Urine ran down his left leg.

"Is something wrong?" asked Ribi.

"I have to go rest." Don Giovanni left quickly, without looking back. But he knew there was a puddle on the floor. Ribi would have to clean it—Ribi, who kept cleaner than a virgin on her wedding morning. Mortification drew his lips back tight against his teeth in distaste. He loathed being himself. All he wanted was to throw off those revolting clothes and burn them.

Burn, like the urine. For oh, it had burned again. Worse this time.

By evening, the burn was like fire. Every time something passed his lips, even the smallest thing, even the tiniest taste, the urge came and the pain increased. Control of this one simple bodily function had become an illusion. He drank wine until he couldn't lift the jug anymore. He heard terrified screams as he fell asleep, and he knew they were his own.

When All Saints' and All Souls' Day finally came, Don

Giovanni was weak and thinner than ever. He hadn't dared eat in days. He drank only when his mouth became so parched, he thought he couldn't breathe anymore. And then only wine, because it dulled the pain.

Don Giovanni closed himself into the Wave Room. The only person he allowed in was the servant who brought a fresh jug of wine. And then he'd turn his face to the wall, so the man didn't know. A nose might suspect, but without eyes to confirm, the man couldn't be sure.

His trousers grew stiff with caked blood. They cracked with every movement. The hard creases sawed away at his groin and thighs when he walked. He had become the most disgusting creature he could ever imagine.

Heavy tapestries had been hung over the Wave Room windows to hold in the noise of his screams. Musicians were located nearby on every side to mask those screams.

It was good the boy artist hadn't shown his face. Don Giovanni wouldn't want him to witness this. The artist had treated him like a man. He couldn't stand it if those clear gray eyes acknowledged him as a monster.

He peeked past a tapestry now. The courtyard profusion of people and food and flowers and wine and music and animals—yes, animals; Don Giovanni had let it be known that animals were welcome this year, too—that profusion nearly made him smile. He let the tapestry drop and stepped back into the center of the room.

"The feast is going on," Don Giovanni hissed through gritted teeth to the air he felt sure was listening. After all, the timing of this latest affliction was too awful to be an accident. He refused to let anything be ruined by his illness, whatever it was. This feast belonged to everyone. "You can't ruin it." He raised his fists high in front of his face. "I know you're behind this. You see how close I'm getting to winning. You rose in fury. But you're not the only one who harbors fury. I will not take off these clothes. I will not wash!"

The urge came. And he hadn't drunk even a drop. He doubled over. His member would split apart at the pressure. "Out!" he shouted. "Out, out, damnable waters!" Blood and urine and tears burst from him. He collapsed on the floor.

Pain exhausted him. His body was too heavy to lift. He lay motionless. "At this rate, I'll die before the three months and three days have ended. You'll lose." If only he could laugh. A part of himself stared down on that body and shook its head. No one would believe he had once been the most renowned lover of Messina. He didn't believe it himself. He passed out from the pain.

Don Giovanni woke with a start. Water whooshed up his nose. He was drowning. He pushed himself up on his elbows and blinked against the sunlight. The tapestries had been pulled down from the windows. Sun glittered in the water that puddled beside him.

"Drink." Ribi held the jug to his lips.

Don Giovanni jerked his head away. "I can't."

"You have to."

"It will make it worse."

"It's the only way to make it better. You should have told me." Ribi made a tsk and shook his head. "You should have told me as soon as the blood started."

Don Giovanni managed to get to a sitting position. "Go away. I don't want you to see this. I don't want anyone to see this."

"Did I rid you of the worms?"

Don Giovanni squeezed his eyes shut. He wished he could squeeze his ears shut. He wished he could squeeze out the world beyond his skin. "Yes," he whispered.

"Then trust me. Let me help you."

The rim of the jug pressed against Don Giovanni's lips. He drank. The urge came, the pressure, the intolerable pain, the explosion. He screamed and pushed Ribi away. But the man came crawling back, holding the jug, pressing it to his lips. Ribi's remarkable persistence prevailed even as Don Giovanni's screams and thrashing grew more violent.

It took a week of drinking water almost continually, with fruits between glugs of the liquid, for the sickness to pass entirely. But then it was gone. Vanished.

Don Giovanni was left with blood-thickened trousers, but healthy innards once again.

And none too soon. The morning after his first good night's sleep since the illness began, the king's messenger returned. Don Giovanni heard him on the road. He looked out the north window of the Wave Room and saw a wagon loaded with sacks. On the front bench were two men. And on horseback in front of the wagon was the king's messenger. His black broad-brimmed hat made him unmistakable.

The king was sending a gift. A gift in return for Don Giovanni's gift. An act of friendship. Nothing could be better. They understood each other, of course; he should have expected it. They'd both had to fight for their independence. The messenger must have been astute and told the king of Don Giovanni's remark about understanding throwing off shackles. What could be a more natural foundation for a friendship?

Panic fluttered Don Giovanni's insides. Last time, the messenger had insisted that he speak alone with Don Giovanni, without the palm screen. He'd probably do that again. But he mustn't see Don Giovanni's trousers. How could he hide them without making it obvious what he was trying to do? He hurried to the kitchen.

"Ribi, we have a guest. Pull that side table out from the wall. I'll stand behind it. You load it with offerings. Things that smell strong."

By the time the servant who let the messenger in found Don Giovanni, his lower half was hidden behind a table piled high with pungent cheeses and meats. "You have a guest, sire."

"Show him in."

But the messenger was already entering. He moved with the same assurance he had last time. And the same graciousness; if he noticed anything worse in Don Giovanni's appearance, he gave no hint of it. He bowed. "The king thanks you for your generosity."

"I thank him in return for allowing it." Don Giovanni opened his hands toward the food in front of him. "Please have something to eat."

"It does look delicious." The messenger hesitated only the briefest moment. It would have been customary to sit at this point, but no bench was available. He filled the empty plate Ribi handed him and cut cheese with his knife, eating it off the tip politely. "Marvelous," he said. He ate quietly for quite a long time. Then he put down his plate and dipped his completely clean fingers into the finger bowl. He looked Don Giovanni in the eye. "Your generosity is infectious, you know."

Don Giovanni didn't know how to respond. It wasn't entirely clear whether this was a good or bad remark. He waited.

"Others heard of your contribution and added their own. The king has more than enough to build the cathedral."

"I'm gratified to hear it."

"So I've brought back a wagon of your gold."

Not a gift. Not an act of friendship. Useless gold. "I won't take it." Don Giovanni pressed his lips together to keep them from trembling. Then he sighed. "Please tell the king it would be an insult to me to return such an insignificant gift. If he doesn't want the money, you should keep it. You and the two drivers of the wagon."

The messenger looked surprised, but he bowed more deeply than before and left.

Don Giovanni heard the wagon rumble away on the coastal road. He closed his eyes against tears. He stayed in the Wave Room for the rest of the day and night.

Early the next morning, Don Giovanni took a walk through the fields behind the villa. The chill was brisk enough to make him walk more quickly than was comfortable, given his now rough trousers, but not strong enough to keep him indoors. Cani ran ahead of him and disappeared into the woods beyond the stubble.

His eyes were still heavy with unshed tears. The king had wounded his pride yesterday. It was funny that he had any pride left, actually. Pride was a stupid emotion. It was time to give it up.

"Hello, there." The call came from behind him. "Please wait."

Don Giovanni stopped and turned.

A woman hurried after him. She came so quickly, her shawl fell back from her head. Black curls cascaded down her shoulders. Her bulbous cheeks were almost obscenely rosy. Her breasts strained against the worn cloth of her dress. She threw herself at his feet.

Don Giovanni pulled back in alarm. Was she hysterical?

"Oh, my master. I've found you."

He looked around. There was no one to hear, no one to see. This couldn't be some kind of cruel joke then. So the woman must be mad. "You've mistaken me for someone else, madam."

She settled back on her heels and looked up at him adoringly. "You're Don Giovanni, aren't you?"

"I am."

"Then there's no mistake. I've heard about you. I couldn't come to the feast, though I wanted to. I've wanted to meet you for over a year."

"Here I am," he said softly. Maybe he was feverish, but if this was delirium, he might as well enjoy it.

"I've come to offer myself."

Yes, this was delirium, but it couldn't have come at a better time. His groin was healthy again. It responded appropriately.

She smiled shyly. "I don't mean it so coarsely as it sounds. You gave me everything worth having. In return I'll give you what little I have to offer."

"I don't recall giving you anything."

She shifted her legs around to the front and pulled up her skirts just enough to reveal the inside of her right calf. The act was decidedly modest, and as a result that much more seductive. Don Giovanni bent forward for a better look. A red scar cut a circle in her flesh. She'd been branded. His stomach turned.

The Romans of centuries past branded their slaves. Often on the face, but with women on the shoulder or upper arm, so as not to mar their beauty if a Roman lord wanted their company. Somewhere back there some emperor or other had changed the branding to feet and legs. This poor woman's master had kept up the barbaric tradition.

"He's not my master anymore. Thanks to you."

A freed slave. Full of gratitude. Delirium would have been much better. What a hideous history she must have. Don Giovanni swallowed his sadness. "Get up, please. What's your name?"

"Call me debtor, for I'm in debt to you."

"You don't owe me anything. Really."

"I know. Everyone knows. You ask nothing in return. When the king sent back the money he didn't need, you refused it."

News traveled fast. Don Giovanni looked down at his bloodstained trousers. He should have stayed hidden in the Wave Room.

"You don't have to keep those trousers on. Not with me. You don't have to hide anything from me. Tell me what you want."

Her voice was so soft, like the subtle sweetness of clover honey. He had to strain to hear it. The voice of a woman who had suffered. It was everything he wanted. Everything good and pure.

She smiled. "You want more. Don't be afraid to tell me. Or, better, just take." She got to her feet.

Don Giovanni couldn't hold in a gasp at being this close to a beautiful woman.

"There's a stream up this way. It's barely a trickle at this time of year, but it's enough. You can shed those awful clothes and lie in it."

Lie in cold water.

"My hands will keep you warm."

"I can't." Don Giovanni's voice barely came.

"Of course you can."

"No. I can't wash."

"Silly man." She put her head down and looked up at him through her lashes. "I'll rub you everywhere. You don't have to do a thing. I'll make you clean. Then we can be together. You can do whatever you want with me."

Her hands on his wretched flesh.

"I can see the man behind the hair, behind the rags. You aren't wretched to me. You're handsome."

In dreams women had said that to Don Giovanni, but he never thought he'd hear it in the waking world. What could it hurt to share a kiss with this woman?

"As many kisses as you want."

"Just one." One blessèd kiss. Don Giovanni held out his hand. "Take my hand and come kiss me."

She laughed, but nicely. "After the stream. Please. After the stream you can have whatever you want."

Lying in a stream. Being rubbed. Passive. How could that count as washing?

Her eyes flickered past him and returned, anxious.

Don Giovanni looked where her eyes had gone. Cani was coming toward them. The dog approached in a crouch, his lips curled back. He snarled.

"Don't be afraid," Don Giovanni said to the woman.

"Stop him." She backed up.

Cani barked now.

"Hush!"

But Cani was out of his mind. He barked so ferociously, his paws left the ground. He circled them.

The noise hammered in Don Giovanni's head. He could hardly hear himself saying "Hush." Now the woman would be afraid. She'd leave. She'd leave with all her kisses still on her lips. He'd be alone again.

"Yes, I'll go if you don't get rid of him," she said.

She heard him, above Cani's racket. She heard his thoughts. He went over what they'd been saying to each other. It was hard to remember, hard to be sure, but he could almost swear she'd been talking to his thoughts as much as to his words all along.

How close he'd come. Yet again.

He fell to his knees in gratitude and disappointment.

"Stupid fool! Did you really think anyone could believe you handsome? You're a vile lump of excrement. You always will be." A laugh lingered in the air. The woman was gone.

Cani whimpered. He sniffed where she'd been. He nosed his way under Don Giovanni's heaving chest and howled as the man sobbed.

Another Portrait

THE MESSENGER RETURNED ON 8 DECEMBER, DON GIOVANNI'S twenty-third birthday. But this time Don Giovanni had no false expectations of a gift. The king had not befriended him. Besides, no one knew the significance of the date.

He came alone on horseback, making a neat trail in the first dusting of snow.

"The king is a young man, as you know." The messenger was uncomfortable today. He turned his hat in his hand. "He hasn't married yet."

Everyone knew that. Why should the messenger be anxious at saying something everyone knew?

Don Giovanni looked away again, distracted, on his cushion throne. Though it was his choice not to tell anyone it was his birthday, he still felt cheated that no one knew, no one celebrated.

He didn't want to be here listening to this messenger's insipid words.

"So he has no daughters," the messenger went on at last. "But he and the queen mother are very much impressed with your service to them."

It had been a long morning. This was Don Giovanni's third visitor already. He was tired of hearing how impressed everyone was with him. He yawned. Then he rolled slowly off the cushions, each movement sending jabs of pain in places he'd rather forget about, and got to his feet. He stood by the window, his legs splayed because the sores had returned now that winter offered no flower petals to heal them, and opened the shutters wide. For once he didn't care that a breeze might carry his stench back to the messenger's nose behind him. This man seemed to have the nose of a stone. And eyes, too. He never showed revulsion at being with Don Giovanni.

Maybe he didn't exist. Maybe he was something concocted by Don Giovanni's ever-weakening brain. Don Giovanni should ask Ribi.

The sea was turgid today. The little cove that had drawn Don Giovanni to this villa in the first place jumped alive with white caps.

When he'd woken this morning, he'd made the final calculations. Three years, three months, three days from 1 November 1169: the fateful day was 4 February 1173. The fourth anniversary of the wave, and the Feast of Saint Agata. The realization didn't surprise him. Indeed, it came like expected news, like something he had been born to know.

Only fifty-eight days remained. After that, people wouldn't have to lie when they said they were impressed with him.

"Are you listening, sire?"

"Vaguely." Everyone said the same thing, so what was the point of listening closely?

"Then let me repeat. The king has no daughters. But he and the queen mother are grateful for your service to them. They wish to give you the hand of the king's eldest sister."

Don Giovanni turned to face the messenger. His ears filled with pressure, like the feeling of being underwater. Water over and under and all around him. Oh, on 4 February he would dive underwater. He would dive as deep as he could, no matter how cold the sea was. Right now, though, the pressure in his ears increased uncomfortably. Maybe he'd implode, become a blob of stinking slime at this messenger's feet. "The hand of the princess?" His voice sounded metallic, saying those utterly stupid words. But what else could he say? Never would he have predicted this offer. Could it really be true?

"The elder princess. Yes."

A bride. A wife. He thought of saying he wasn't worthy of this honor, the insincere standby phrase of the haughty, but the messenger was bound to secretly agree. And it wasn't true. Why shouldn't Don Giovanni have a wife? People treated him as a beast, they thought of him that way. But a creature's measure was internal, after all. And even a beast needed someone; everyone needed a companion.

A wife. A beggar, a princess, he didn't care. Someone to talk with. To kiss with. A wife. One woman for the rest of his life. That's all he needed, all he longed for. A best friend, the love of his life.

And there was no one else to arrange a marriage for him. Why not let the king do it? A laugh rose in his throat. He stifled it with difficulty; he didn't want to spook the messenger and ruin the whole offer. He put his hand over his mouth to hold in stray jabbering. Yes, control was possible.

"His Majesty is too good." Don Giovanni attempted a small bow. "With humility, I accept the honor."

"Then I will take the news back to the palace. I'll return as soon as a date has been set." The messenger left quickly.

Don Giovanni heard his heels click on the steps. He heard the door open and close below. He watched the messenger collect his horse and mount. His senses took it all in while his thoughts stayed numb. By the time his brain woke again, by the time he realized he had to be part of choosing the date, to make sure it was after the Feast of Saint Agata, the messenger was already galloping away.

He sank to the floor.

He could send his own messenger to say the wedding had to be after 4 February. In fact, it had to be a week after that. Two weeks. He would need time to recover. He picked at the red patch of skin on his forearm. The itching in his head and back and bottom and thighs didn't even elicit scratching from him anymore, it was so unremitting. Now and then he'd slap hard at it, but scratching was futile. A month, then. He would ask for a wedding date in March.

But no. Waiting might be a mistake. It would give the princess time to think about things. She might hear about him—about his smell, his filth. She might refuse.

No. No, he had no choice. He would stay in his villa until the messenger came back with the wedding date.

If the date was too soon, the princess would be horrified at the wedding ceremony.

Well, he'd simply stay hidden. He could participate in the ceremony from behind palm fronds. Or maybe he'd have a screen built, of lacquered wood, painted beautifully. She'd wonder, but she wouldn't be afraid. After the wedding, he'd stay at a distance until he had a chance to transform. She'd be amazed when she saw him. He would sweep her off her feet. That was something to look forward to.

If she didn't hear the truth about him from someone, or somehow catch a glimpse of him, or a whiff of him. If she didn't run away immediately.

This sort of thinking could drive a person mad.

If he wasn't mad already.

A wife. Out of nowhere, a wife.

He couldn't lose her. Not before he had a chance to prove

himself to her. Here and gone. That would be too cruel. Like the boy artist—coming and going. A friend lost. But losing a wife, that would be the cruelest thing yet.

What a birthday.

Don Giovanni went to the side table and drank directly from the jug. The only way to wait was in a drunken stupor. But the wine didn't help this time. It only brought images of a young woman, her face shrouded, shocked, screaming, crying, railing. He threw himself on Cani and fell asleep, clutching the patient dog.

Three days later, the messenger returned, followed by a coach. An elaborately carved and painted coach, drawn by a horse with a red hood and white rings painted around the eyeholes. Don Giovanni watched from the window. His breath stopped. The royal coach. The king was in there. Or the queen mother. Or maybe even the princess herself. This couldn't be good. If they saw him . . .

He went as fast as he could down the stairs, down, down to the wine cellar. Waddling, he stumbled halfway and fell. The cold floor bit at him. The damp air entered his bones and set him shivering. He wanted to hide behind a barrel, but there wasn't room, so he crouched between two.

Voices called his name from one direction, then another. Now Cani barked. They'd enlisted his dog against him. Unfair cleverness. Cani would never betray him if he understood.

The dog's nails clicked on the stone, like the messenger's heels clicking behind him.

"Sire, are you there?"

Cani wiggled happily in front of him. The dog's tail moved in a circle, he was so excited.

His position was clearly untenable. He cut a ridiculous figure. Don Giovanni stood up as straight as he could manage. His bride was here and gone. He'd lost her.

"I've brought someone to meet you."

"I don't want to meet anyone."

"This person is an artist." The messenger pulled his cloak tighter. "There's a chill down here. Shall we go upstairs to talk?"

An artist had come in the royal coach? This must be one talented man, to merit such treatment.

Don Giovanni followed the messenger up the stairs, all the way to the Wave Room.

A small man in floppy black trousers stood facing the wall. The long black smock, the wool cap. All so very familiar, so very dear. Could it be? After so much searching to no avail, Don Giovanni had come to think of the boy artist as unreal. If it weren't for the drawing that greeted him every morning, he'd be convinced the boy was nothing but a figment of his imagination.

The boy turned and looked up at Don Giovanni with those liquid silver eyes that spoke to him immediately. At last! Don Giovanni opened his mouth but words stuck in his throat.

The boy artist's eyes pleaded with him. He shook his head almost imperceptibly. What was he trying to convey? And how was it that in this past year he seemed not to have grown at all?

Not a hint of a mustache. And as thin as ever. Except his cheeks; they had plumped out a little. The wooden box lay at his feet.

"This is the artist." The messenger folded his hands in front of his chest, like a priest about to deliver bad news to his congregation. "The princess has requested a picture."

"And I am honored with the privilege," said the boy artist, keeping his eyes locked on Don Giovanni's. "Meeting you is an even greater honor." He bowed that laughably low bow.

But Don Giovanni didn't have time to wonder why the boy was pretending they were strangers. He reeled under the disastrous news. He was doomed. "A portrait of her groom," he said icily to the messenger.

"Nothing so elaborate as a portrait. A drawing, shall we say."

"Did you describe me to her?"

"Not at first, no. But she heard rumors. You know how Palermo is. They upset her. So she asked me."

"And you complied," said Don Giovanni with a hint of accusation, though he knew he had no right to feel that way. This man owed him nothing.

The messenger spread his hands, palms up. "I am a man of few words. But true words. What could I do?" He shrugged. "The princess prevailed on the queen mother."

Don Giovanni took a deep breath. "And if the princess doesn't like what she sees in the drawing?"

"I don't know. Kings don't break their word. But . . ." The

messenger let his hands drop by his sides in defeat. "She's a girl who gets her way." He looked to the side table.

"Help yourself," said Don Giovanni with resignation.

The messenger poured a glass of wine and drank it slowly. "Draw something clear," he said to the boy artist. "Something that will satisfy her." He turned to Don Giovanni. "I'll return at the end of the day to take the artist home." He bowed and left.

The two of them stood facing each other. Silent.

"I'm back," said the boy, finally.

"I tried to find you."

"I didn't want to be found."

"Why not?"

"Friendship has costs."

"And we were friends?" Don Giovanni whispered.

"You knew we were. We are. I couldn't pay the price."

"What price?"

"My freedom."

"I don't understand."

"I don't want you to understand. Just believe me when I say it was hard for me. Your company that day was a pleasure. To be able to talk openly, without hiding who I truly am—a rare treasure."

"Who are you truly?"

"An artist." He put up his hand in the hush sign. "Please. Find it in your heart to let this matter lie. Find it in your heart, please, to forgive me, even though when this drawing is done, I'll be gone again."

The boy's face was so solemn, Don Giovanni's heart ached. "Just so," he said softly. "Well, now, we have work ahead. Another drawing."

The boy blinked, almost as though he were blinking back tears. "I'll use vellum this time, if you want. Sheep vellum. It's better than goat."

"And colors?"

"Maybe. I haven't decided yet." The artist stretched vellum over a wood frame and tacked it in place. He picked up a charcoal stick. "It's cold today. Shall we stay inside?"

"Where?"

"Why not this room?"

"The Wave Room."

The artist's head bobbed in recognition at the words. "Oh, of course. You named it after the wave of Messina." He tilted his head at Don Giovanni. "The wave that changed your life." He left the vellum and charcoal on the floor and walked along the walls, trailing his fingertips over the blue tiles, just like Don Giovanni did sometimes. His eyes wandered appreciatively. "Who put these tiles up?"

"Giufà."

The artist stood before a twist of deep blue, white blue, and green blue sweeping up from the floor into white spray near the ceiling. He folded his hands behind his back. "I've never heard of him."

"So what?"

"Are you questioning my credentials again? I thought we were past that. I've heard of the best artists."

The back of Don Giovanni's neck itched horribly, but he wouldn't scratch it. He wouldn't take the chance of inflicting on the boy the thought of what it was like to be him. "You mean the best in Palermo."

"I mean the best in Sicily. And on the mainland, too."

Don Giovanni almost smiled. "There you go, giving me your credentials. I thought we were past that."

The artist laughed. He walked again, still trailing his fingertips along the wall. "He has strength, while not giving up precision or flow."

"Listen to you. Such a grand artist. Would you rate him among the best you've seen?"

"It's hard to judge from one work. But the difficulty of making something that moves you when you're working with variations on but a single color—that demands skill. He's made the sea here, the calm and the wild. The power. I think maybe he is among the best."

"Then you haven't heard of all the best artists, have you?"

The artist gave a cockeyed smile. "You win."

"The walls in the Story Room were done by Paperarello. Bet you haven't heard of him, either."

"No."

"Want to see?"

The artist followed Don Giovanni into the next room. He stood open-mouthed in front of the mosaics. "These are fairies and witches and talking horses." He spun around to face Don Giovanni. "Are you reliving your childhood tales?"

"Normally this room is full of children, playing games or listening to a storyteller or singing. But from the week before Christmas till the end of the holidays, everyone is busy with family events. Storytelling won't resume till mid-January."

"Oh. Well . . ." The boy touched a line of gems. And another. He walked all around the room three times, always returning to one talking horse. Then he did the strangest thing; he pressed a cheek against the horse head. "It's stunning." His arms stretched out to each side; his belly and chest and legs hugged the wall. Like a starfish with only four arms. Was this ecstasy Don Giovanni was witnessing?

After a while, Don Giovanni spoke softly. "And the ceiling in the dining hall was done by Quaddaruni. Come."

The artist reluctantly detached himself from the wall and followed Don Giovanni. But when they came into the dining hall, he lay on the floor and studied the ceiling. Silent.

He stayed so long, Don Giovanni felt foolish standing. So he lay down, too. Immediately, he gasped. "You're right. The effect is even more spectacular from this perspective."

"How did you find them?" whispered the artist.

"They came to me. Just like you did. I let it be known that I was interested in good work. And that I'd look at anyone's work. You didn't have to be famous."

"And you recognized how good they were."

"Are you surprised? You're the one who said my choosing you was credentials enough. Was that just flattery?"

"More a way to keep the discourse on course." The boy gave a quiet sigh. "Tell me about what happened?"

"What do you mean?"

"The wave. Tell me."

So Don Giovanni talked. He told about being a spendthrift and losing all his wealth. About the walk down the coast, then inland to Randazzo. About gathering snow for nobles' desserts and then the spring and summer and autumn of working outdoors. Then a change in his fortunes, money he hadn't expected. And the long year of being homeless, but able to buy food, and, oh, the wonderful company of Cani, and finally the luck of buying this villa.

He didn't mention the devil or the white linen purse.

They lay side by side, not speaking anymore. The air between their chests and the ceiling shimmered with Don Giovanni's words. He could feel their weight, but they didn't crush him. Breath came easy.

"Will you be eating the midday meal with the rest of us today?"

Don Giovanni sat up.

Ribi stood at a respectful distance.

"Not me. But maybe this artist . . ." Don Giovanni turned to him. "What's your name, anyway?"

"Make one up for me."

And it suddenly struck Don Giovanni: this boy knew much about him now, but he knew almost nothing about the boy. His spine prickled. Friendship had balance—true friendship, that is. His skin tightened with wariness. Cani had attested that this was not the devil. But the devil had assistants, and Cani might not react to them. Assistants could be anywhere, anyone.

And he had to admit it, they had nothing in common, no basis for a friendship. Why on earth would a lithe, graceful boy befriend a stinking beast?

Wait a minute now. They had appreciation of art in common. That was firm and sharp.

The devil's hook, perhaps?

Don Giovanni pushed himself up on his hands and stood unsteadily. It was 20 December. Only forty-six days to go. Nothing could make him lose now. He wouldn't allow it.

"The boy artist can eat with the rest of you. I'll take my meal in the Wave Room."

"No, please." The artist scrambled to his feet. "I'll eat with you. Please."

And so they ate together, Don Giovanni sitting on his cushion throne and the boy on the floor.

When they finished, the boy took up his vellum and

charcoal and drew. He drew all afternoon. At one point he went to his box for paint. Then he continued working.

And the whole time, no one spoke.

"You're angry with me," said the boy at last. He put away the paintbrush and the charcoal. He cleaned his hands on a towel from his box. "What did I do?"

"You've told me nothing about yourself."

"You haven't told me everything about yourself, either."

"But you've told me nothing. Nothing at all."

"You know my father died."

"And your mother finds your persistence annoying. That's it."

"Ask," said the boy.

"What's the most important thing about you?"

"To me or to others?"

A good question. The kind of question that Don Giovanni would have asked now—but never in the old days. The kind of question the devil would know Don Giovanni would find enticing. "To you."

"I'm an artist."

"To others," said Don Giovanni.

"To my family, I'm a fool."

"And to those outside your family?"

"I'm rich."

So they did have more in common. That's why this boy artist came in the royal coach. He was nobility. Don Giovanni swallowed hard. "To me?" he murmured.

"You can answer that better than I."

"Try."

"I like you."

Don Giovanni's throat narrowed. Breath hurt. "Why?"

"You use your wealth wisely. Everyone knows what you do. I knew before I came here the first time. I listened to all the things you've done in the year between. But today, now that I've looked at the work by the artists you've hired, I understand it better."

"So it's because of how I spend money? A political matter."

"Hardly. Or I wouldn't call it political. It's hard to explain. It's more . . . it's more that you know why you do these things."

"Why do I do them?"

"You understand."

"What?" asked Don Giovanni desperately. "What do I understand?"

"Suffering." The boy licked his bottom lip. He'd done that the first time he came. Don Giovanni recognized it now as a sign of anxiety; it made him feel protective of this callow soul. The boy lifted his chin. "You are humane. Tender. Dear."

Don Giovanni pitched his head forward between his legs to keep from swooning.

"Are you all right?"

"No. But I'm going to be. Soon." Don Giovanni looked at the boy and held out his hand. "Can I see today's drawing?"

The boy handed over the vellum.

A hair ball filled the sheet. The hairs were so fine and so many that they formed a kind of cloud. Like the smoke clouds that hung perpetually over some of Mount Etna's craters. This was the mess that was his head. This was what the world saw.

But, just as with the last drawing, the more he looked, the more things took shape under the hair. A hint of this and that. Were his lips really that full? Was his jawline that strong, his nose that straight? Nothing was definite except one eye. It peeked out, shining with black paint on white. Stark. Unrelentingly honest. The eye of a man.

Gratitude nearly stole his voice. He murmured, "Thank you."

Two weeks went by. Don Giovanni stood by the window pulling his hair to ease the pain in his skull, when the messenger rode up on his horse. Don Giovanni leaned from the window and shouted even as the man was dismounting, "Tell me. Tell me this very second. Will the princess have me?"

The messenger ran to stand under the window and puffed his hot breath into the morning chill. "The elder princess said no."

Don Giovanni gripped the window ledge. He knew it. The artist's drawing was too accurate. His cheeks went instantly slack; they hung like jowls. Maybe his flesh would fall from the bone.

"But you're lucky not to have her. The younger princess has agreed to marry you, and she's a much nicer lass."

"The younger princess?" Was this a dream?

"If you don't care about a fancy ceremony, you can be wed tomorrow."

"Tomorrow? The fourth of January? No. No, we must have a ceremony. A big one. In two months. The fourth of March."

"I don't know if it's worth the wait."

"I do."

"May I come in?"

Don Giovanni closed the shutters and hurried down the stairs. There was a younger princess. A second chance. And she'd said yes. How could it be? How could he be that lucky?

He met the messenger midway on the stairs.

The messenger took off his hat and bowed. "I don't know if the king and the queen mother really want something grand. I'm sorry."

"They fear they'll be embarrassed. But they won't be."

The messenger shook his head. "Small affairs can be intimate. Just the royal family. Especially since the younger princess is marrying before the elder."

"All right," said Don Giovanni. What did it matter, anyway? "A small wedding. But afterwards a huge reception, here at my villa. I'll invite the guests." He had so many people he could invite. All his servants and their families. All the children who came to storytelling and their families. The artists and artisans who had worked on the villa. The boy artist, in particular. He could be Don Giovanni's best man. He was the tender one—he was so very, very dear.

Oh yes, many people would be happy to celebrate the wedding with him. "The king and the queen mother and the elder princess, they don't even have to come if they don't want to," said Don Giovanni.

"They might well not."

"I understand."

"The fourth of March," said the messenger. "I'll convey the news." He turned and went down the stairs. At the bottom he looked back. "Congratulations, sire."

Congratulations. Everything was going right. But "Wait!" Don Giovanni stumbled after the messenger, who was already out the door.

"Wait!"

The man turned.

"What's her name?"

"Your princess? Miriam. But she goes by Mimi."

His princess. His own princess. Mimi.

Hope

ZIZU'S NOSE DRIPPED. IT SEEMED LIKE NOTHING. A TYPICAL January cold. But then his septum grew a white membrane. He held one hand over his sore throat. He sat in the corner of the Wave Room and didn't want to go anywhere, do anything.

That wasn't normal. That was as far from normal as possible. Zizu always bounded with energy. When he had a cold, Giancarlu used to have to scold him to slow down, take it easy. And after Giancarlu left to join Kareem in opening a meat market, Ribi scolded Zizu. The boy was constantly in motion.

Don Giovanni paced. He had a servant go out to the mountains to bring back snow, so Ribi could make Zizu special desserts. But the boy only smiled wanly, gave a listless lick or two, and fell asleep.

Within days the children who came to the Story Room, the

regulars, had the same symptoms. Their parents stopped bringing them.

On the fifth morning Zizu developed a fever. It wasn't high. It didn't make Don Giovanni's hand jump away when he finally dared to touch the boy's forehead, but it was definitely there. And the boy stopped eating altogether. When he opened his mouth, drops of blood showed on his tongue.

Reports came in that the other children were the same. They sank into a malaise. Rapid pulse, stupor. Most of the older ones recovered quickly. But Zizu, who was among the oldest, got worse. He developed a swollen neck—what the surgeons called "bull neck." Don Giovanni longed to rock him—this sweet, sweet child, in such pain. His arms ached from the need to soothe Zizu, but he couldn't be sure the child might not revile his touch, even as sick as he was.

Then the younger children got bull neck, too. The younger they were, the sicker they got. When one of them fell into a deep sleep he couldn't be woken from, the dreaded word spread: *diphtheria.*

Palermo had been struck with an outbreak of one of the most virulent childhood epidemics. Desperate parents came to Don Giovanni's villa. They stood outside his door and called him down.

"It started here."

"What?" But the next instant he understood. He would have

expected this if he had allowed himself to think about it. "I keep out of the way. Far from anyone. Hidden."

"I've seen you before."

"And our children catch glimpses of you slinking around."

"You're a walking cesspool."

"And everyone knows cesspools are the source of diphtheria."

"It started here. With you!"

Don Giovanni shook his head vehemently. He had already sent men to Termini Imerese, to the east along the coast. They brought back healing mineral waters to the afflicted families. He paid for surgeons to visit them all. He sent pots of hearty stews thick with meat to their homes. Not because he thought the illness was his fault. No. He never drank from the same vessels the children used. He never went near the only fountain in the villa. He steered clear of the well. Water was too attractive to risk being near it.

The one child he'd ever really been physically close to was Zizu. And he hadn't touched even Zizu until after the illness started, when he'd wanted to feel the fever for himself. Just that one time. He couldn't be responsible for the epidemic. It wasn't possible. He couldn't be harming all those children he cared about. He couldn't be harming Zizu. His Zizu.

So he'd done those things simply because he wanted to help. He had to help.

He shook his head harder and harder. Nausea rose in his throat.

"Clean yourself up, man."

"Cut your hair."

"Shave."

Don Giovanni held out his hands to quiet them. "I'll have the villa scrubbed from top to bottom. Then swabbed with vinegar."

"But you, you're putrid."

"You have to wash yourself—not just this place."

"Three weeks," said Don Giovanni. "That's all I ask. Go away for three weeks. When you come back, I'll wash."

"Our children could all be dead by then."

"Let me through." A man stepped forward from the back of the crowd. He carried a bucket. "Start now." He threw water on Don Giovanni.

"He's right. Where are the buckets?"

"In the kitchen, I'm sure."

They pushed past him.

You cannot wash yourself, change your clothes, shave your beard, comb your hair. You cannot wash yourself.

Don Giovanni hobbled around the outside of the villa, chanting inside his head.

"Stop right there!"

"What's he muttering?"

"Madman."

"Cani," he called. "Cani, Cani."

The dog came running from the woods, a black stream of barks crossing the fields.

The crowd had kept its distance from Don Giovanni anyway. But now it backed up farther.

"Hurry with the buckets."

"He's getting away. Hurry!"

Don Giovanni hobbled faster. He checked over his shoulder in terror. Ribi burst out of the villa and ran to catch up with him. Cani now patrolled between his master and the shouters. His bark kept them at bay.

Ribi wrung his hands. "Where are you going, sire?"

"Away. It's best you don't know. But keep everything going for me, Ribi. I'll be back in time for my wedding. Make all the arrangements."

"I will, sire."

"There's money in the two wine barrels at the rear of the cellar. Keep sending food to the families of those children. Do whatever you can to help heal them."

"I will."

"Don't let Zizu die. Please."

"I'll do my best, sire." Ribi wrung his hands harder. A tear rolled down his cheek.

"I know you will. I'm sorry I said that."

Water flew at him. Another bucket. A third. Drenched, he hobbled across the dry, half-frozen field, toward the woods.

Zizu mustn't die. No children must die. It couldn't be his fault. His filth couldn't be that destructive. No, no, no.

He trudged along. The floor of the pine groves was spongy with dry needles. They pierced his skin, but he felt nothing. Blood filled in his footsteps.

No children must die.

He remembered when he'd closed himself into the inn, the week before he bought this villa. He'd worried then that Zizu and Kareem and Giancarlu, the boys who depended on him for food, might starve. But he closed himself away anyway.

It was different now, though. He loved Zizu. In a more generalized way he loved the other children, too. And he loved Ribi. And he loved the boy artist. Maybe that's who had started all this flood of love: the boy artist.

How ironic that love had given the devil his fatal weapon.

Zizu. Zizu had been by his side since he first came to Palermo.

Don Giovanni ran, stumbled, fell. Cani stopped and whined in his ear.

"This won't be a real win!" Don Giovanni shouted at the air. "Killing the children voids it. Do you hear me?"

A wind came up. Branches rubbed against each other in sad groans.

He remembered the shape the devil assumed when he came as a man. His fine clothing. His noble diction.

"Shabby behavior! Shabby, do you hear? And you try to

present yourself as refined. You talk about not being crude. Killing children is as crude as it gets. If a single child dies, you forfeit. Do you hear me? I win automatically. Do you hear me?"

He quivered inside his wet clothes. "It's you versus me. I yield the villa. I yield whatever comfort it offers. I'm totally exposed. Come on, come at me with whatever you've got. But if you go after the children, you lose." He held his fists in front of his chest. "You and me. That's all. This is our battle."

The wind died. Nothing stirred in the woods. No birds. Nothing happened.

He got up and walked.

The devil said Don Giovanni's pathetic little rules didn't bind him. But some rules had to be universal. He grabbed faith and held tight. The alternative was too grim.

He walked slowly, his head high.

January was the coldest month. Even at its coldest, though, this part of Sicily was mild compared to the frigid winters of Mount Etna. A man wouldn't die of exposure here, no matter how wet his clothes were.

He wouldn't consider trying to find Kareem and Giancarlu. Both were too old to pick up a childhood disease, but harboring him would bring the crowd's wrath down on them.

He had his purse on him. He always did. So he could buy a room at an inn, if someone would only open the door to him.

He headed west, staying in the woods. Trapani was the next-largest town in this area. Maybe he'd even go to Erice, where his favorite winemaker was. He'd be okay. There were only three weeks to go.

He slept that night in the woods, curled in a ball with Cani. Like the old days. Except that in the old days Cani was a bit younger. The dog had gotten used to sleeping inside, warm and dry; he cried. But he rested his loyal head on Don Giovanni's chest and slept fitfully.

In the morning Don Giovanni told Cani to go home. He'd been selfish to take him along. Besides, he could do this on his own now, for the mere thought of marrying his princess, Mimi, could keep him alive. But the dog wouldn't leave, even when Don Giovanni shouted at him. Even when he threw rocks. Of course not. He got on his knees and apologized and cried as he hugged the beast his very love had marked for the devil's torture.

The next night passed in the woods, too.

On the third morning, their need for fresh water couldn't be denied any longer. They followed a footpath out of the woods. By afternoon they looked out over a wide gulf, where a small port town nestled at the foot of a mountain. Monte Inici. Don Giovanni could hardly believe it. He walked so poorly these days, they had covered hardly more than half the distance to Trapani, though they'd traveled nonstop for nearly three full days.

They went directly to the public well. Women with their heads covered stepped away quickly. A Muslim town. Good.

Muslims never denied the needy. Don Giovanni made a bowl of his hands and stretched them out, pleading.

The women shrieked in fear at man and dog. They huddled together talking rapidly, then ran off.

Don Giovanni looked into the well. The rope hung flaccid. They'd taken the bucket.

His dry tongue rasped against the inside of his cheeks. Water. What could he use as a container?

He broke a branch off a shrub, tied it to the end of the rope, and lowered it into the well. When he brought it up, he and Cani licked the wet leaves. It wasn't enough.

He took off his smock. This wasn't washing. This was wetting. There was a difference. He freed the linen purse from the threads that held it tight to the inside of the smock and tucked it into the waistband of his trousers. Then he tied the smock to the end of the rope and lowered it into the well.

When he pulled the sopping cloth up, he twisted it over his mouth, over Cani's mouth, wringing out the water. And memories of blood. And all the rest. The water tasted ancient, like death. He dunked the smock over and over. Until it caught.

Don Giovanni stopped pulling immediately. He leaned over the well, but it was impossible to tell what held the smock. He gave the rope a small jerk. Then another. He tugged a little harder. Then harder still. And the rope came up. With nothing attached.

He used a stick to try to snag the lost smock. Nothing. It was as though it had disintegrated.

He turned and slid with his back against the well wall to the ground. The rough rock ripped at his already raw back. He cried, while Cani licked his tears.

It wasn't the cuts. He had so many cuts and sores.

And it wasn't the cold. He could dig a burrow under pine needles, as he and Cani had done for the past two nights. And the days, they were fine. If he moved quickly, or as quickly as he could, he would fight off the shivers.

It was that everyone could see his scabrous self. His smock had shielded him from that, though piteously.

And oh, Lord in heaven, what if he was, indeed, the cause of the diphtheria outbreak in Palermo? What if he'd now infected this town's well? He had to tell someone.

He ordered Cani to stay there, and he walked down the path to the first house he found. He knocked.

A man opened the door.

Don Giovanni suddenly didn't trust himself to say the right things. Tears threatened to come again. He wiped at his eyes.

The man closed the door. A few minutes later he reopened it and held out a shirt.

"Thank you, but I can't accept it. Thank you," Don Giovanni managed.

A woman's voice called from within. The man reached

behind him and now held out a large flat bread with a blob of fresh goat cheese on top.

Don Giovanni took it with both hands. "Thank you."

The man started to close the door.

"Please," said Don Giovanni. "Do you know about Palermo? Are the children still sick there?"

"They thought they had bladder of the throat. The bad swelling that causes suffocation. But it was something else. It passed."

"And no one died?"

"No one died."

"Not a single child?"

"No one."

"Thank you."

Don Giovanni went back to Cani. They shared the bread and cheese in equal portions. The man couldn't stop crying. He cried between bites. He cried as they walked west, into new woods. He cried as they curled up for the night. He cried with his eyes shut. The children of Palermo were safe. Zizu was safe. The sweet sorrow of gratitude finally carried him off to sleep.

It took an additional two nights in these new woods and most of the day beyond that before they arrived in Trapani and knocked at the door of an inn that backed on to the hill.

The shutter upstairs opened. "Who's that?"

"Don Giovanni."

"Don Giovanni of Palermo?"

Don Giovanni fought the urge to cross his arms over his chest to try to hide his shameful exposure. It would have been a futile act. "Yes."

"The one who brought diphtheria? I can see it. Look at you. Disgusting mess. Get out of here. Leave Trapani. We care about our children."

"It wasn't diphtheria. No one died. It was something else."

"Really? How do you know that?"

"Everyone knows that," Don Giovanni said as forcefully as a hungry, thirsty man could.

"Even so, you're hideous. No one would come to my inn if I gave you a bed."

"Please just sell us food then. Set it outside the door. I'll leave money there."

The innkeeper shook his head.

"I'll leave double what the meal is worth. And if you'll fill an amphora with water for us, I'll pay triple for the food, plus an extra gold coin for the amphora." It was an exorbitant price.

The innkeeper closed the shutters. Fifteen minutes later, he opened the door and set a cloth parcel and an amphora outside.

Man and dog wandered down the long sickle-shaped beach, sat on the cold sand, and ate and drank.

"We'll be all right, Cani. We've both got fat on us. If we can eat every third day, like we've done so far, we'll be all right. Only sixteen days to go. Then we'll get ready for the wedding. My bride. Your new mistress. We can do this."

A cold wind whipped off the sea with no warning, spraying them, ruining their bread. They ate it anyway.

They walked south, staying as close to the shoreline as they could. That night they dug a hole high up on a beach and slept while the wind screamed over them.

In the morning Cani whistled and snorted and threw himself around to get free of the sand.

Don Giovanni had to wipe sand off his eyelids before he could open them. He picked crusts of sand from his nostrils. He blew sand from his lips. He wondered if he should try to scrape it from his chest and back, but he had nothing to scrape with. The wind blew hard, grinding the sand deeper into his skin, throwing it in his eyes.

They kept following the shoreline, anyway. It was the shortest route to Marsala, where they arrived on the third morning. Cani whimpered continuously. And every part of Don Giovanni stung except the center of his chest, where he'd clutched the empty amphora tight.

The flat land was perfect for agriculture. To the north of the city was a river, where Don Giovanni and Cani drank their fill. The water sloshed in Don Giovanni's stomach as they walked to the first farmhouse and paid the farmer for a hearty meal.

"I've got an old smock," said the farmer, filling the amphora with the delicious local wine.

Don Giovanni hadn't asked for wine. Cani didn't drink it, after all. But both man and dog had already had their fill of water, so he didn't object. But the smock . . . ah. "Thank you. But I can't accept it."

"The wind's unusual this year," said the farmer. "No one remembers anything like this. The oldest man in town says that when his grandfather was a child gales cut through like a sword. But that old man makes up things all the time."

Don Giovanni nodded. "The wind can hurt."

"Well, you can sleep with the horses if you want. You won't find anything better around here. Derelicts like you aren't tolerated."

Derelict. That's what he looked like, for sure.

"In the smaller towns south of here they kill people like you."

That couldn't be true. The king's laws extended all over Sicily.

"Go on, sleep with the horses. In the morning, you can have bread in goat milk. A traveler needs a hearty start to his day. And maybe you'll have changed your mind about the smock by then." The farmer gestured toward the stable. "Go on now."

The offer was good. Too good.

They couldn't accept.

This was the final stretch. Don Giovanni had to expect traps everywhere. Thirteen days to go.

"Thanks. But we can't stay."

The wind followed them down the coast, driving sand into every exposed opening in their bodies. When a wagon would pass on the road up the slope, they'd flatten themselves into the sand. That farmer could have been the devil's assistant, or he could have simply been a friendly man. But it wasn't worth the chance. There was still one more large town on the western coast. Don Giovanni and Cani wouldn't stop till they got there.

It took four days before they finally arrived in Mazara. They should have made it in three. And they would have, if it hadn't been for the wine. Being drunk slowed a man down. And made him stupid; Don Giovanni dropped the amphora as they were coming to the edge of town. It broke on a stone beside the road.

Mazara was smaller than Marsala. Still, it was big enough for the residents to know how to treat strangers—or it should have been. Instead, the people here were immediately suspicious of him. No one was tempted by the offer of huge sums of money for food. No one seemed moved by the plight of the needy, though Don Giovanni was sure the town had plenty of Muslims. The inlaid street pattern gave that away, and the white houses.

Don Giovanni and Cani wandered hopelessly along a road. Four days was too long to go without water. They'd never make it through a fifth. They'd be dead by night.

They came to a date palm tree and rested under it. Don Giovanni closed his eyes. He could fall asleep easily.

Death was such an easy option.

Smack!

His eyes popped open. He grabbed his aching upper arm. A half-desiccated orange lay on the ground beside him. The skin was clear yellow with just a touch of red tinge.

"Get away or I'll throw more. And take that evil dog with you." The man was hard to understand. He was dressed in white robes and had only two teeth showing.

Don Giovanni looked at that yellow fruit, the color of hope. He let his mouth hang open. He made his eyes go vacant.

"Idiot!" The man threw another orange, *thump*, at Don Giovanni's forehead. "Don't show your dirty face on the holiday. Disrespectful. Disgraced!"

Cani attempted a growl. It was hardly audible.

Don Giovanni put a calming hand on the dog's head. He swung his own head from side to side.

The man threw a third orange and a fourth. *Smack* on Don Giovanni's bare chest; *thump* on his rag-covered knee. But that was all; the thrower's sack hung empty.

Don Giovanni picked up the oranges and held them like a baby to his chest. "We're going. Come, Cani." He limped. The dog staggered.

They went back to the road they'd taken into town. No one was on it. So Don Giovanni sat and tried to peel an orange. The peel was tough, though, because the fruit was past ripe. He got up and walked back to the place where he'd dropped the amphora. The shards still lay by the rock. Don

Giovanni summoned every drop of strength he had left and gouged an orange with the point of a shard. He held the dog's mouth open and squeezed in what juice there was. After all, Don Giovanni had had wine for the past few days, but Cani had had nothing.

When the juice was gone, he used the shard to cut the orange into pieces and he and Cani devoured the sour flesh. They did the same with the other three. Then they spent the afternoon walking in the country outside the northern part of town, going from orange tree to orange tree. Most had been picked clean, but now and then an old fruit hung from a high branch. And fairly often there were rotting ones on the ground.

"Nine nights to go," the man crooned in the dog's ear. "Then we prepare for Mimi."

They went back to the road and crossed through the town, and Don Giovanni burst out laughing. A river came down through the middle of Mazara. If they'd only walked a little more to the south, they'd have found it that morning. They drank, though by now their thirst had been satisfied. They drank because a river should never go unappreciated. Then they walked past one of the most beautiful mosques Don Giovanni had ever seen.

That night they slept in a hole they dug on a beach south of town.

Don Giovanni knew of no other towns of any decent size along the coast to the south, but scattered villages were everywhere. He'd have to use his judgment and trust people he thought might help.

They went back to Mazara first, though, and followed the river up, beyond the brackish mouth to where it was fresh and clear. They drank and Cani swam. And a woman washing her laundry gave them a flat bread to share. So charity still existed, just not on a holiday.

They walked the coastal road until it ended. Donkey paths took its place, winding inland. Don Giovanni followed any path that wasn't too steep for their flagging energy. The sparse vegetation promised nothing. They ate bitter leaves and hoped they weren't poisonous.

At nightfall they came to a terraced bit of hillside. The farmhouse showed no candlelight, no lamplight. Knocking on a door in the middle of the country in the dark was tantamount to asking for a beating, so Don Giovanni went back to the terraces and pushed himself against a dirt wall to sleep.

Cani watched him, then wandered off.

Well, that was all right. The dog would be there when he woke. He always was.

Don Giovanni slept.

Cackling woke him. Chicken noises. Then a shout. More shouts.

Don Giovanni clutched the amphora shard in his hand—it was his only weapon of defense—and ran down the terraces away from the farmhouse. He ran and ran until he couldn't hear anything anymore. He panted in the pitch black of night.

Something moved off to his right.

"Cani? Cani, is that you?" he called softly.

The dog appeared at his knees. A dead hen dangled from his mouth.

They ate it together, every edible bit. Only the feathers, beak, and claws remained.

They walked in a large arc past the farm in a generally southern direction. When he could barely put one foot in front of the other, Don Giovanni dropped in his tracks. "Let's sleep, Cani."

They curled up together.

"Stealing is wrong," Don Giovanni said to the dog. "Good dog. Stealing is wrong."

The next day they spotted another farmhouse soon after waking. It must have been around noon. Don Giovanni went right up to the door and knocked.

No one answered.

If he went in and was caught . . .

He sat in the shade of a tree. It was a pleasant day. Spring had definitely come to this part of Sicily, though by his reckoning it was only 28 January.

28 January. One week to go. One week.

He heard the men before he saw them. They were talking about how Beppe's chicken coop had been raided.

Don Giovanni clamped a hand around Cani's muzzle to keep the dog silent. He peeked around the tree trunk. Three men walked along a path leading a donkey. He hid behind the tree again and waited until they had gone into the farmhouse.

"Come on, Cani." They hobble-ran across the vineyard.

They walked all day long, staying as far from people as they could.

That night they came to a river. This was a wide one. It ran with the swiftness of first spring. They drank. Then Don Giovanni caught elvers in his hands. Elvers so early. He hadn't eaten them since his spring on Mount Etna. They were tiny, but plentiful. Don Giovanni and Cani slept with full stomachs.

They might as well stay here now. There was food and water and no one to chase them away. Besides, Don Giovanni was loath to keep traveling farther and farther from his Mimi. So they hid out there the next day and night.

By chance, a passing peddler stopped at the river the third day. He told them a group of farmers was hunting chicken thieves. He looked at them knowingly. Then he told them to keep going south, along the coast, and they'd get to the town of Sciacca. It wasn't far. They'd find good people there. People who would take care of them. The peddler repeated his words several times, as though Don Giovanni must be a half-wit.

Anything could be a trap. Anyone could lay it.

But the prospect of people who would take care of them was too alluring to put aside. And if the farmers were really hunting for them, they had to get on the move again. Five more days. Five more nights.

They walked on inland paths, but always within sight of the sea. They walked all day. They slept off the path, behind a bush.

The next day they continued. They came to the village of Sciacca in the early evening. Not even a village really. A cluster of homes. They knocked on a door at random.

The girl who answered was neither pretty nor plain. Her eyes took them in calmly. "How much money do you have?"

A completely unexpected question. Don Giovanni swayed on his feet. "How much do I need?"

"A full recovery is expensive."

A full recovery? The words dazzled like precious stones. Whatever she meant, he wanted it. "I've got it."

"Show me."

"Bring me a meal, big enough for me and Cani—lots of meat. And I'll fill your hands with gold."

The girl shut the door.

Don Giovanni looked around. A woman leaned out the window next door and stared at him. Two men stood in a doorway across and down the path, watching him. Eyes probably fixed on him from every home within sight.

He went back the way he'd come until he couldn't see the houses anymore. Someone might still be watching, but he didn't know where from. And it wasn't yet dark enough to be sure they couldn't see.

"Sit, Cani."

Cani sat.

Don Giovanni sat in front of Cani and wrapped his legs around the dog.

Cani made a low rumble in his throat and turned a quizzical eye on him.

Don Giovanni stealthily pulled his purse out of his waistband and laid it on the small patch of ground between his crotch and Cani's. "Dear one," he whispered. "Give me money. Enough for the full recovery."

The purse filled and overflowed. Gold spilled from it.

Don Giovanni tucked the purse back in place. He rolled his trouser cuffs to form little pouches that he filled with gold. Then he and Cani went back to the girl's house.

This time a woman answered. "Have you got the money?"

"Have you got the meal?"

The woman went back inside and came out with a large bowl full of stew.

Don Giovanni reached for it.

"No." The woman put it on the ground. "Here."

Cani stared at the bowl and whined.

Don Giovanni picked up the bowl. The pungent smell made his head swirl. He nodded toward his legs. "Reach into my cuffs for the money."

The woman's lip curled. "I won't touch those pants. They have to be burned."

Don Giovanni shook each leg until the coins fell onto the ground. "We'll be back in the morning for another meal."

"All right."

"And this money pays for the recovery, too," said Don Giovanni, acting as though he knew what he was talking about.

"Of course."

Did he dare push his luck? "The full recovery."

"Of course. We can start it tonight."

"No. Give me four more nights. Then we'll start it. From now till then, I'll come by morning and night for a meal."

"The sooner we start, the better."

"Good night."

Don Giovanni walked back along the path, then off into the shrubbery. He set down the bowl. Dog and man ate side by side. They slept unmoving, heavy as trees.

The next day, Don Giovanni carried the bowl back to the house. The girl answered this time. She poured warm goat milk into the bowl and put a stale loaf of bread on the ground beside it. Don Giovanni carried the food to the shrubs where they'd slept the night before. He broke the bread into bits and dropped them into the milk. He and Cani ate side by side again. They slept on and off all day. In the early evening they brought the bowl back for more stew.

That night it rained. In the morning, Don Giovanni and Cani lay in mud. The sun hardened it on their backs. It cracked off as they walked to the house.

The girl opened the door. She came outside with a large sack slung over her shoulder. "Follow me."

"What about food?" Don Giovanni held the empty bowl.

"Put it down," she said in annoyance. "Follow me." The girl led them along a path and soon they came into a real town. How foolish Don Giovanni had been, to think those first few houses were the whole of it. Sciacca had not only a mosque, but a Christian church. And lots of homes.

The market square teemed with vendors calling out their wares and produce, and shoppers haggling over prices. A man fried large pieces of dough in sizzling oil over an open fire. Don Giovanni stopped at a wall and secretively pulled out his purse. When he had a coin in his hand, he slipped the purse away again and bought two pieces of the dough. He and Cani ate in large sloppy bites.

Now he realized the girl was gone. She'd disappeared into the crowd. "Find her, Cani," he said in the dog's ear. "We want the full recovery. We need it."

Cani wove through the tables of cheeses and meats and cloths and yarns, with Don Giovanni close behind. There she was, waiting.

"Hurry," she said.

They walked through town fast. Don Giovanni struggled to keep up. He couldn't risk losing sight of her again. Her and that heavy bag. A full recovery. They went up into the foothills of a mountain.

"Where are we going?"

"Monte Cronio, of course."

"What's there?"

"The cure." The girl frowned. "That's what you came for, after all."

"But not yet. Two more nights. Just two more nights."

"Two days from now I have to travel to Agrigento. My cousin's getting married the day after—the seventh of February. I can't wait. If you want my help, you have to start today."

"No." Don Giovanni stopped. "If three days from now is the seventh of February, today is the fourth of February. But that's wrong."

"No, it's not."

"Today is the second of February."

"You've lost track of time," said the girl. "It's easy to do, in your condition. I've seen illnesses like yours play tricks on people's minds all the time."

Don Giovanni had been careful. He'd counted off the days. He couldn't be wrong. "I'm not ill."

"Yes, you are. You came for the cure."

"I'm just dirty."

"Call it whatever you want. Just hurry."

Up ahead the mouths of caves opened wide, as though calling. And were they calling? Don Giovanni could have sworn he heard voices.

He did. Happy voices.

He followed the girl into the first cave. Naked men leaned over fissures in the rock, where steam came through. They talked to one another about how strong they were getting, how well the vapors from the hot springs underground were healing their insides, how soon they'd be back home and running things again.

Somewhere in Don Giovanni's distant memories was a whisper about this place. Monte Cronio. Yes, it was well known for its therapeutic power. Had those old memories been in charge all along? Had they brought him here?

"Take off your trousers."

"No."

The girl made a tsk. "I've got the towels in here." She dropped the sack onto the ground in front of her feet. "If you want me to soak them in the healing waters and rub you down, I have to start now. You're a bigger job than most."

"No. Two days from now."

"I already told you. I can't wait two days."

"Then go away."

"You won't get your money back."

"I don't want my money back."

"I have bread in here, too. With fried onions and mushrooms on top."

"It's not mushroom season."

"My mother dries them in the fall. We have them whenever we want. They're the big yellow kind."

His favorites. Zizu often gathered them for him.

The girl opened the sack. She took out a cloth bundle and untied the knot. Onion and mushroom scents joined the hot vapors.

No. Don Giovanni smiled. His favorite mushrooms. Ha! "What a pathetic thing is evil." He walked out of the cave and climbed up into the mountain. Behind him came the smallest, highest note. A keening voice. As he and Cani climbed, the voice grew into a wail, a shriek. The wind joined it. Hail fell through the sunny sky, smacking him hard, knocking him senseless.

It was early dawn when he woke. A freak snowstorm had come to Monte Cronio. Who said the devil was hot?

Don Giovanni clutched Cani and waited. "Mimi," he said. "Mimi, Mimi, Mimi. Mimi awaits if I can make it just one more day, one more night." He closed his eyes and spoke to the yellow haze of hope inside his heart. "I will be everything good I can be for this Mimi. I'll never make her sorry she married me. I will cherish her. For the rest of my life. I promise. If I only get the chance."

Yellow

ON THE MORNING OF 4 FEBRUARY 1173, DON GIOVANNI WOKE more frozen than not. He and Cani slip-slid down the mountain to the cave. He leaned over fissures in the rock and let the hot steam warm him.

It was over.

He could barely understand yet what it might mean. Over. Done. Won.

He took off his trousers and rolled the purse up small in his fist. He whispered to it, then held up a gold coin. “Who will shave my hair off?” he called out.

Sciacca turned out to be a good town for a full recovery. By the end of February, Don Giovanni had healed everywhere. His scalp was free of pus. His skin was thick and olive again.

His hair had grown back to a short curl. He looked young—not boyish, there was a definite solemnity to his eye—but young again. Healthy.

He wore the best clothes Sciacca could offer, which weren't bad at all.

He rode the best horse Sciacca could offer, almost directly north, through the hills and mountains, all the way to Palermo. Cani ran along beside. For that reason he had to go more slowly than if he'd been alone. By the evening of 2 March, he and Cani arrived at the villa.

Ribi answered the door. He looked from Cani to Don Giovanni, back and forth, back and forth.

"It's you!" shouted Zizu from an upstairs window. He waved wildly. "It's Don Giovanni!"

"Sire?" said Ribi.

Don Giovanni grinned.

The men hugged.

Zizu came running out and jumped into Don Giovanni's arms, closing his legs and arms around the man's chest.

Every servant in the villa lined up to shake the master's hand. But Don Giovanni hugged them all.

Ribi had been true to his word. *Marzapane* in the shape of tiny brides and grooms hung all around the courtyard.

They spent the day of 3 March burning the cushions from the throne in the Wave Room and putting in a matrimonial bed.

On 4 March, Don Giovanni went to wed the younger princess, Mimi, in Palermo's cathedral. The old cathedral, as it was now called, ever since Mimi's brother, King William II, had made known the plans for the new one that would be built at Monreale.

Mimi looked glorious in her long gown. Yellow. How on earth could she have known the color of all his hopes?

She fluttered down the aisle like a butterfly. When the veil was lifted and her lips appeared, her tongue ran along the bottom lip in a familiar way. Don Giovanni was amazed and then, on second thought, not amazed at all to find his bride was the artist who had drawn his hands as birds, who had seen the humanity in his eyes.

Tender and dear, indeed.

He raised an eyebrow.

"I played the boy artist outside my brother's castle," she said clearly, though others might hear. "And the retiring princess inside."

Of course. The former could persist only so long as the world of the latter was unaware. Art was not for a woman's hand, despite the occasional German nun, and they were considered daft, after all. But when her sister had asked for a drawing of Don Giovanni, Mimi stepped forth and offered to go in disguise—what they thought was a new disguise—as a boy artist. Don Giovanni could imagine the scene. It all fit.

"No need for disguise anymore," murmured Don Giovanni.

"For either of us," said Mimi.

Is a wager with the devil worth it? Who can ever know what might have been otherwise? But today was his wedding day. Don Giovanni set aside the unanswerable question in favor of what he did know, in favor of the only holiness he could count on—a yellow butterfly, a breath of hope, the love of his life.

A Note to the Reader

"DON GIOVANNI DE LA FORTUNA" IS AN OLD SICILIAN FAIRYTALE. All versions of it that I've found are not set in any particular time period and are quite short—two or three pages. Some are available on the Internet, including these sites:

www.surlalunefairytales.com/bearskin/stories/dongiovanni.html

www.pitt.edu/~dash/type0361.html#sicily

I chose to start this story in the late twelfth century because that was a time of important transition, political and cultural, trickling down from the Sicilian nobility to the ordinary people. The foundation for later reforms can be traced to these years.

I chose the specific year of 1169 because I wanted a jump start for Don Giovanni's loss of wealth, and I found it in the massive eruption of Mount Etna that year, with the ensuing earthquake that leveled Catania and the tsunami that washed over the walls of Messina. I wrote the first few chapters of the first draft of this story in December 2004. Then I took a couple of days off from writing to enjoy Christmas with my family. The day after Christmas, a major tsunami caused devastation and tragedy in the countries on the Indian Ocean. The coincidence stunned me. I couldn't work on this story for a long while afterward.

When I picked the story up again, I promised myself there would be no more natural disasters in it. (Working on fairy tales can induce a strange sense of connectedness between events that one's intellect knows are disparate.)

Because of the time frame I've imposed on this fairy tale, the princesses had to be the sisters of the king rather than the daughters as in the traditional tale. King William II at that time was just a young man himself.

I also chose to end the tale at the wedding, while the traditional tale goes on to tell of the anger of the queen and the older sister at the younger princess's good fortune in marrying such a handsome man after all. Both women met terrible ends, from going blind with envy and drowning in the sea to losing their souls to the devil. To me, this was Don Giovanni's tale, and, while I very much hold dear the frame of any fairy tale, it would have been a worse injustice to sully it with their demise.

Acknowledgments

Thanks to Robert and Barry Furrow, and Libby Crissey, Robbie Hart, Angela Repice, Bill Reynolds, Richard Tchen for comments on earlier versions. Thanks to Bryan Miltenberg for his meticulous checking and to my strong-stomached, kindhearted, and persevering editor, Reka Simonsen, for everything else.